In Pursuit of Happiness

Short Stories

David Kimel

I want to build a bridge to you,

To help you find me and my thought,

To taste, to touch, to see my view

And feel my love, when I'll be not.

David Kimel

Contents

A Few Words About the Writer David Kimel

Writer David Kimel has already made a name for himself among readers in both Romania and Canada—the country that has adopted him and where he has chosen to live for several decades—through his numerous works. Without claiming to list them all, I would mention A Foggy Sunrise, Simple Seeds, A Sweetless Love, and the book at hand: In Pursuit of Happiness.

Before expressing any thoughts on his literary endeavours, I'd like to highlight a remarkable quality of Mr. Kimel's character that I've come to appreciate—his discretion. It defines him as a truly special person. There is nothing of the loud, self-important bravado so often in fashion these days. Mr. Kimel does not seek attention through ostentation, nor does he make waves. He brings his books quietly before the reader, seemingly careful not to offend anyone, expressing gratitude to all—without fear that doing so might somehow diminish his reputation.

With a rich background in journalism at Observatorul (The Observer) magazine in Toronto, and an even richer life experience—lived intensely and often requiring him to overcome difficult challenges—Mr. Kimel reveals himself through his writing, which stands out for its deep analytical insight and, not least, its refined and intelligent humour. We are thus introduced to a man for whom seriousness, modesty, common sense, and perseverance are core moral values. These have always guided him, and this reality is metaphorically and sincerely conveyed in the pages of this book:

"As if driven by the wind into the open sea like a ship with full sails, I had to navigate carefully, avoiding rocky edges surrounded by foaming waters, striving to remain calm in the turmoil that could have claimed my life. And now that I've reached this resting place near the final page of the album, when I look back to the beginning, I ask myself—was I the one who charted these journeys, or was it someone else? If it was me, why would I have chosen such winding paths among steep ravines and thorny climbs when it would have been so much easier to walk smooth, straight roads? Of course, it wasn't I who chose the path, but fate. It was fate that forced me to take each step, confronting obstacles in search of a more peaceful place. Or perhaps it was Providence."

In Pursuit of Happiness is a symbolic opening to this collection of short prose, foreshadowing, through its symbolism, some aspects of the author's own life. A fractured flight of a generation that nevertheless found the strength to carry on—at times forced into exile simply to survive. The framework of stories, along with all lived or heard experiences, touches on common issues faced by the Canadian diaspora. Through a fluid and natural writing style—marked by warmth, clarity, and originality—David Kimel brings to life eras, characters, and situations with an exceptional sense of proportion. His writing seeks to inform without shocking, to stir thought without causing distress. He contributes to the important act of remembering, an idea I mentioned earlier.

Placed at the beginning of the book, the author's note of thanks brings this idea into sharper focus while also serving as an invitation to read:

"History is not written by the great leaders of nations from across the ages, but by those who lived through the times and left behind testimony of the heroic acts of their forebears. We, those who toil with pen in hand, are merely witnesses to the events we've lived through—trying to recount them as faithfully as possible for those who come after us. Our reports, chronicles, and stories are simply each of our responses to the events unfolding around us—events that, in one way or another, affect us all."

And so, I, too, extend this invitation to you to read. I wholeheartedly recommend Mr. Kimel's book—and books—and congratulate him on this fine achievement.

Irina Constatinescu

In an admirable way, the writer David Kimel offers each of us, through the reading of this book, a mirror in which we clearly see the enduring human experiences: love, joy, peace, pain, fear, anger, courage, pride, guilt, shame, acceptance, and forgiveness.

With striking simplicity, he intuits just where to place a spark to ignite emotion and feeling—and the interaction with each character in his short stories gives us pause for thought.

At times, the reader is merely a silent witness to the unfolding events on the stage of the book; at other times, they are drawn into the role of a character swept up in the whirlwind of actions that ripple through not only the present but also the hearts of those involved. It is a journey that captivates with its ups and downs, an adventure in search of treasures buried in the caves of the past— a past the author stirs to life in order to share it with his accomplices: the readers.

Daniela Cupșe Apostoaei

Gratitude and Appreciation

The mysterious journey of life that has led me to pause today in this shaded little corner before an album filled with many photographs has wound its way through slopes, valleys, forests, and meadows. Yet nowhere along the path did it allow me a moment of rest, joy, or reflection—except in recent years, when the fruits of my labour began to gather. As if driven by the wind into the open sea like a ship with full sails, I had to navigate carefully, avoiding rocky edges surrounded by foaming waters, striving to remain calm in the turmoil that could have claimed my life. And now that I've reached this resting place near the final page of the album, when I look back to the beginning, I ask myself—was I the one who charted these journeys, or was it someone else? If it was me, why would I have chosen such winding paths among steep ravines and thorny climbs when it would have been so much easier to walk smooth, straight roads? Of course, it wasn't I who chose the path, but fate. It was fate that forced me to take each step, confronting obstacles in search of a more peaceful place. Or perhaps it was Providence.

For as long as I can remember, my path has been decided by others—those older and more experienced. I was told what to do without being asked if I wanted to, and I complied. Only later, after the first quarter of my life, did I rise to declare that it was enough!

All this must end now! But by then, it was too late—the path had already been laid, and all I could do was continue along it, even though what I truly longed for was an entirely different journey and a different destination. I did what I had to do, not what I desired, but I tried to do it well, and everyone was happy.

When I arrived in a foreign land, what I had been trained to do under the socialist 5-year planned economy that had helped me support my family—was of no use in the free world society. This realization of my luck of qualification, sent waves of shock through my entire body. Suddenly, I found myself like a bird without feathers, and out of shame, I had to borrow false ones to cover my nakedness. I had to pretend I knew how to do certain things I never have done before. Even though I knew I was an impostor, being a good observant of the meticulous work of true professionals, I began cautiously to imitate them—and succeeded. At times, the fear of being exposed, of not being able to solve problems or provide the right answers, drove me to search, to study, and to learn what I did not yet know. My sleeping hours were plagued by nightmares. In the end, my effort was recognized, and no one questioned the expertise I claimed.

After retiring, I continued to work as a consultant. With more time on my hands, I recalled the other path—the one I was never allowed to take in those early years of searching. Applying the experience I had gathered over time, I realized that words, like the parts of a well-thought machinery, can be assembled to form a harmonious whole, where images, feelings, and thoughts, can give rise to moving stories.

I began to write. Timidly, in a newly learned language—so that my children and descendants could read—I wrote my first verses. In those early attempts, the friendship and encouragement of kind souls helped me immensely, offering thoughtful feedback and corrections. Thus, my first poetry collection, *Simple Seeds,* and the autobiographical novel *A Foggy Sunrise* came into being, both published some years ago.

It is my belief that none of these efforts would have been possible without the help of my family and the extraordinary people who encouraged and guided me with their advice and the warm generosity of their friendship. Among them, I must mention Mrs. Camelia Ciovică, Professor Dr. Tiberiu Șeicaru, Dr. Mircea Diaconescu, and Mrs. Victoria Dimonie. In Toronto, the friendship of poet Veronica Pavel Lerner and author Elena Buică has been— and remains—a sun that lit up many moments of doubt about my early writings. I must especially bring thanks to Anca and Dumitru Puiu Popescu, editors of *Observatorul Magazine*, who encouraged me, published my first poems and then printing my columns in the magazine for nearly 20 years.

I must also acknowledge the support I received from writer

and award-winning documentary filmmaker Daniela Cupşe Apostoaei and graphic artist Codruţ Miron, who edited and designed my short stories book *Anişoara*, published in Romania. My journalistic work extended to several magazines in Canada, Israel, and Romania thanks to distinguished literary personalities such as Leonard Voicu, Adrian Grauenfels, and Nicolae Băciuţ, who generously featured many of my creations in their publications. I thank you all.

Finally, my collaboration with Paramount Book Publishing—especially the editorial team led by Mrs. April Woods and Gary Miller—has filled me with immense gratitude. They helped me bring to life the novel *A Sweetless Love* and now this new book, *In Pursuit of Happiness*. For their execution, professionalism, and artistic insight, I owe them a debt I can never repay—except with my heartfelt love and sincere respect.

David Kimel

In Pursuit of Happiness

1

She was just his classmate. Always the same every day, he timidly walked past her and sat down on one of the back benches without anything ceremonial to attract the attention of others. That's how Mihai was all the time: silent, discreet, not demanding. He was nicknamed Picasso because he drew beautifully, with shadows, like in a photograph. Sanda also nicknamed Moțata (Tufty), at that time, did not really look at Mihai. Not that he wasn't likable, but other boys in the class, and even the upper classes, were much more attractive than him; they had more charm, and all the girls swarmed around them. But all that happened back then, years ago, when they barely looked up to see what was going on around them.

More than a dozen years had passed since then when they happened to see each other again around Christmas at a mutual friend's family home in New Haven, Connecticut. Sanda had just gotten a position as a chemist at Hartford University and was living with a lady friend who worked there. Mihai traveled home from a conference in New York, and on his way to Toronto - his hometown - he remembered the friends he met in the refugee camp in Greece, where he and the others were waiting to receive their immigration visas. He thought of stopping by to see them, and there he found the house full of guests. Sanda was also there, but at first, they didn't recognize each other. He was now a pleasant, tall man, dressed in an elegant suit that fit his athletic body impeccably, and Sanda had become a woman who gave the impression that she knew she was discreetly noticed by men. Only after realizing that everyone else knew each other, feeling isolated, did they realize that they also had known each other for a long time, since high school.

"Weren't you called Moțata in school?" Mihai asked her

"Wait a minute: Picasso? You?"

The surprise of this meeting would change both of their lives. Mihai had become an architect. In Canada, after a few engagements with some private firms, he decided to work on his own, building villas for lucky business clients who wanted to flaunt their new social position. You could say he was successful. New clients called on his services, and he became known and appreciated for the style of his constructions discreetly associated with the surrounding environment that distinguishes the buildings without provocative ostentation. He was honest and imaginative and had found several collaborators who executed his projects on time and in an economical spirit.

After a trip from Toronto to Niagara Falls, he started to promote the idea of building a bridge across Lake Ontario to connect metropolitan Toronto with the city of St. Catherine on the opposite side. This bridge could shorten the road by about 60 kilometers between the two cities without considering the savings in time and fuel achieved by its construction. It was a bold idea that required huge funds, but the economic advantages at the provincial level could not be overlooked, and the initial investment could be recouped by paying for its use. There were comments, lots of articles about the project and congratulations, but like many other projects, it ended up forgotten in the drawers of some politicians preoccupied with more urgent problems.

Gaining respect among the guild, he built himself a tasteful home in a residential area on the outskirts of town. The grounds encompassed a line of centuries-old trees and a picturesque stream meandering along the bottom of a valley that gives the place more poetry. Among the friendships formed among his new neighbors, Grieg, a bachelor who had a Victorian-style house, had become closer to him. Mihai bought his land from him. After meeting Sanda again, Mihai described the whole story to Grieg one day.

"Do you want to marry her?" Grieg asked.

"I might. We are both from the same place, only one street apart, so we have the same tastes and ideas. She is studious and works at university. We are the same age and have never been married. I think she's right for me."

At the time, Toronto was considered Canada's second, or perhaps third, largest city, after Montreal and perhaps Vancouver.

After the frenzy of Francophone nationalist movements in Quebec that threatened to separate the province from the rest of Canada, most firms established in Montreal, that great cosmopolitan city, moved to Ontario. Toronto's population skyrocketed in a short time, far surpassing Montreal's. Many opportunities have been created for new immigrants, new businesses have sprung up, and the entire region has seen great prosperity. Thus, the province of Ontario surpassed economically and numerically all other Canadian provinces. Compared to the small central Connecticut town of Hartford, Toronto had become a metropolis pulsating with intense cultural activity, luxury shops excelling in gleaming window displays, and lucrative job opportunities.

It was the beginning of the eighth decade of the 20th century. After a visit to Toronto, Sanda was completely captivated by everything she saw and learned from Mihai and Grieg, who took on the role of big brother to guide her when Mihai was too busy. From now on, the topic of their marriage has turned into a top priority goal pursued by everyone with enthusiasm and expectations. On any free day of the weekend, Mihai sought to finish his duties as quickly as possible for another trip to Hartford, where he was awaited by Sanda, from whom he could hardly be separated. Two weekend days were too short because the distance, more than eight hundred kilometers between the two towns, took almost a whole day to drive. Because of this, Mihai started driving almost the whole night to spend more time with Sanda. She could not move to Toronto at this time due to contract obligations with the University of Hartford. Arriving in the morning at the house where Sanda lived with her friend Mimi - her former head of laboratory in Romania - after a sleepless night behind the wheel navigating through the snowdrifts on the road, Mihai could barely keep his eyes open with fatigue. Not even the cup of espresso coffee prepared by Sanda did not help him. He had begun to be exhausted, not only by the road but also by the contractual duties assumed even before meeting Sanda, inherent technical problems, and the need for more money before the wedding.

"Maybe it would be better to fly from Toronto," Sanda suggested to Mihai, seeing how tired he was

"I never know when I will finish what I have to do, and besides that, driving relaxes me," said Mihai.

They decided to have the wedding in August in Hartford because Sanda had more friends than Mihai. She wanted to wear the wedding dress and veil in their presence, take many photos, and send pictures of the occasion to her parents. They found a splendid salon in a restaurant where it was not easy to make a reservation for a wedding; they chose the style of the wedding dress and the taste of the three-tiered cake that would be offered to the guests. Now that all the important things had been prepared ahead of time, all that remained was to let time pass.

On the way back to Toronto, Mihai would have wanted to leave earlier because he had an important business meeting the next morning, but Sanda insisted on staying because that Sunday afternoon, she was invited by a professor from the college to a party and she didn't want to go alone. Mihai went with her. When he finally took Sanda home, turning onto I-90 toward Buffalo, a gust of wind blew snow onto the highway, making the drive dangerous. It was dark, snow everywhere, and there was low visibility. At this time, only a few cars were driving around him. Tired, Mihai tried to dispel his fear of falling asleep at the wheel, slightly opening one of the car windows and increasing the volume of his radio to play louder. As he usually listened to more classical music, he changed the station to something more cheerful and found a trendier song, so he started singing, too. He remembered that after Syracuse, he could cut his way to Canada at the 1000 Islands because, on the Northern side of the St. Lawrence River, there was less snow. It was past midnight, and the road turned to the right in front of him.

When he opened his eyes, he was sprawled on his back in a hospital bed. The walls were white, as were the clothing of those around him, and all over his body, he felt as if he were tingled with spikes all over, as if he were sitting on a bed of nails. He wanted to move but realized he couldn't. His head was fastened in some kind of metal casing that stopped the slightest movement. His hands and feet were inert, heavy as lead, and he found that apart from rolling his eyes, he could practically make no movement:

"Where am I?" he asked

"St. Joseph's Hospital."

"Why am I here?"

"You had a serious accident on the road. You have a fractured spine."

"How long do I have to stay in bed?"

"Weeks, maybe months."

"I can't. I must go. I have obligations."

"Postpone them! You can't move even if you want to. Your vertebrae are compressed. We try to decompress them by traction."

Mihai closed his eyes. After a moment, he opened them again. The nurse with whom he had been talking continued to sit by his bed:

"Am I in Toronto?" Mihai asked her, worried that he didn't remember anything that had happened on the way.

"Not. You are in Syracuse, New York."

"How do I get moved there?"

"For now, you can't. You will be moved after we reattach the ligaments to the back bones and spinal cord. Until then, be glad you escaped your life. Be calm. Try to sleep."

Mihai wanted to ask other questions, but he felt that his strength was leaving him, and following his nurse's advice, he closed his eyes.

2

At first, seeing that Mihai did not answer the phone, Grieg waited until later to find out how the trip to Hartford went this time. He knew that Mihai had important work to finish, so he considered it normal not to find him at home. But when, close to midnight, he couldn't find his friend, he called Sanda to ask her if she knew where Mihai was. Sanda was also surprised that Mihai did not call her all day, but she had no doubt that everything was fine; only the lack of time prevented Mihai from calling her. But now, worried about Grieg's phone call, she saw that she couldn't sleep anymore and rushed to call the police to find out if they knew anything about him. That's how she learned about the accident near Syracuse, where a car overturned on a curve in the ditch between the two directions of the freeway. The next day, Sanda asked Mimi to explain to the university why she didn't show up at the lab and went straight to see Mihai at the hospital.

What she saw there horrified her: Mihai was alone in a large room with a single bed, surrounded by machines and pulleys. He was lying on his back in this bed that looked more like a torturing bed. A metal circle with pointed screws was mounted on Mihai's skull like a kind of crown, the spokes of which joined over his black hair in its center. From this central point, a metal cable was pulled by weights from a pulley mounted outside the headboard. Another pulley with weights pulled the patient's legs in the opposite direction. Mihai was pale, unshaven, motionless like a mummy in which only his eyes and lips could move. A sketchy smile signaled the joy of seeing Sanda, a near and dear figure that, under other conditions, he would have jumped to embrace her. Now, however, he only looked at her leaning over him at the edge of the bed with her eyes drowned by the welling of tears:

"My darling, this misfortune happened because of me. How could I do such a thing? Why did I go to the party that damn night? If I had stayed at home quietly, none of this horror would have happened." Unable to hold back her tears, she began to cry loudly and, sitting on the edge of the bed, buried her head in Mihai's chest.

"No, Sanda, you are not right," he tried to reassure her. "This is not because of you; you are not to blame. Guilt is my destiny; that's what happened to me! Do you see Fate made me come to the party in New Haven where I met you? Fate brought us together after all these years of not knowing each other. And all is destiny! If God wants this, He will make me whole again. What we cannot accomplish now, we will do then."

"No! Why then? What's the point of waiting until then? You are mine now, today. You want me, and I'm yours; no one can separate us! There must be a chaplain in this hospital who can marry us! I don't want to wait!"

"Sanda, my dear, be calm! I might not be able to get out of this bed for the rest of my life. You cannot tie your life to an invalid. Be patient... We still don't know what fate has in store for us."

No Mihai! I am determined. I will call Grieg and Mimi to come here. I'll bring a priest, and we'll get married. Then, I'll apply for my visa to Canada. From now on, you will have me by your side, for better or for worse. Do you understand?"

Mihai didn't comment anymore. Huddled in the white sheets of the bed as if in a sarcophagus modeled on the contours of his body wrapped in sheets, he realized that from now on, he was completely dependent on the will of others, and even if he wanted to resist them, he lacked the physical strength to do that. Before Sanda's arrival, the doctors at the morning visit checked how he responded to external sensors by tickling the soles of his feet and poking him with a needle in various places, but he didn't feel or react to anything. The diagnosis was clear: he was paralyzed from the neck down. Encouraging, the nurse who wrapped him with the sheet told him that this test did not matter and that after decompressing the vertebrae, there was a chance that he would regain his senses as before. Little hope, but still, it was better than nothing.

Sanda watched Mihai's face, the only one that expressed his state of mind, whether he was talking or not, the only one that remained alive and sincere. Of all his vigor, exuberance, and optimism, only his eyes, speech, and facial expression were real in this man to whom she attached herself with boundless love and hope. Now, however, a waxy pallor has replaced the rosy peonies that reddened Mihai's cheeks in the past and darkened his face tormented by suffering.

Mihai, feeling investigated, closed his eyes. Thinking that he wanted to rest, Sanda got up from the bed after a while and left him to talk to one of the doctors who was taking care of him. Mihai was left alone; he reopened his eyelids and, looking at the mechanisms above his bed, he wondered if someone had tried to build a device to help him in his projects, to be able to put on paper the images viewed in his mind, as did in the past with the help of hands? What wonders of science could hold the lines complications of the projects born in his mind? Without finding a clear answer to these questions, his life would have no meaning, Mihai thought. There was no point!

3

Days, weeks, and months passed. The nurse who took care of Mihai was a little right: the miracle of traction, treatment, and medication gave some mobility to Mihai's hands, which could now push the wheels of the wheelchair around the room, not with the palms, but with their bridge from the root of the big finger of each hand. The rest of his fingers were curled up lifelessly like hooks. His legs were could not longer be used either, but the fact that he regained a little mobility in his arms gave him hope that in time, with exercise and discipline, they may also be useful to him in the near future.

From now on, he was no longer at the Syracuse hospital but at his home in Toronto, where several layout changes were made, such as a sloping platform at the side of the entrance stairs, bars along the walls, especially to the downstairs bathroom and the introduction of a hospital bed in place of his former drawing board in his former office at the main floor. The bed was equipped with a crane so that he could be lifted and left on the cart in the morning or on the bed when he wanted to sleep. Of course, these operations were done with the help of other people. Sanda and Grieg were always around him, taking care of him, washing him like a child, dressing him, and helping him eat. Mihai felt like he was in tears when he thought that without the help of these beings, he practically could not have survived. Their help was invaluable, and aware of this, he did his best to cause them less trouble by keeping his demands to a minimum.

The fact that Mihai no longer had to stay immobilized in bed during the day was a real blessing in his life. Now installed in a wheelchair, he could push himself using his arms with limited freedom of movement; he could move from one room to another, watch TV programs with others, or be with them at meals and other activities. This gave him comfort, and in his mind, he regarded these improvements as a real miracle. He could even travel with Sanda and Grieg in his new van, which was equipped with a lifting platform intended for people with disabilities.

The bad part was that he couldn't work like he did before the accident. His last projects were almost finished, and with them, his finances would dry up. What will happen when the money reserves in the bank disappear? All his life, experience, knowledge, and talent with which nature had endowed him could not help now, for his arms could not be raised, could not function, and could not execute any command. All he had was a limited swing of his arms around the wrists at the shoulders and elbows. Usually, they rested suspended on the rubber of the wheels of his easy-to-manipulate wheelchair from one place to another.

Sanda applied for immigration to Canada at the Canadian Consulate in Albany, New York, and was in Toronto on a visitor's visa without the right to work pending a response. Their marriage took place at Syracuse Hospital, and the University of Hartford was understanding enough to grant her a dispensation from contractual obligations, considering her emotional trauma. But the future did not look promising for any of them. A temporary solution came to life with the help of Grieg, who remained a true friend and participant in the drama triggered by Mihai's accident.

Grieg was the sole heir of a family of old English Loyalists who laid the foundations of British settlement in Upper Canada. Toronto at that time was only a minor community formed around a military base, Fort York, near the shore of Lake Ontario. In the early 19th century, when the Americans attacked Canada in 1812, the local garrison and popular militia defended themselves heroically and drove the invaders across the waters of the Niagara River, which separated the American colony from the territory that remained loyal to England. Since then, in his family, every generation, by tradition, especially the men, served in the army with the British troops. Like his own father, Grieg, he chose a military career in which he distinguished himself by receiving the rank of colonel and an important position in the general staff. However, the political envy and unproven accusations of some opposition politicians forced Grieg to resign from the army. Not yet reaching retirement age, Grieg had to find a material source to live on. To begin with, he sold portions of the inherited land, including Mihai's property. Before them, he found some amateurs who bought art objects from his parents' collection.

He soon learned that a new building on Harbor Front Boulevard housed the sale of antique art objects in rented spaces by dealers who wanted to exhibit their artifacts. These sections were separated from each other by framed fences made of wire mesh all the way up to the ceiling. Each section had a lockable entrance gate and contained spaces of various sizes. Grieg decided to rent one of these sections. He carried everything of value from his house and exhibited them there. Paintings, furniture, and trinkets from his parents' house were displayed on tables or hanging on the wire walls. Seeing that many tourists were interested in purchasing them, Grieg began attending various auctions where he bought new art objects to display for sale to his clients. The profit was not negligible.

Sanda, having no other occupation now, enthusiastically accepted Grieg's offer to help him with this venture. Not to leave Mihai alone at home unsupervised, they also took him in the new van with the lifting platform, and so the three of them spent day after day at this place while waiting for another bus with tourists visiting Toronto. With the space being tight, Mihai tried to get out of the way of the visitors who crowded to see the exhibits, asking questions and trying to haggle with the sellers.

In the evening, exhausted after a day of being on their feet, they went home. Sanda, helped by Grieg, patiently undressed Mihai, washed his whole body with a napkin soaked in water, and then Grieg patiently massaged his back, chest, hands, and feet. Many of these operations were done using the crane equipped with wide leather belts to lift Mihai from the wheelchair and carried over his bed. Then Grieg would go to his house, Mihai would stay in his bed with the light off, and Sanda would go upstairs to her bedroom to sleep.

One night, Sanda came downstairs wrapped in a bathrobe and sat in bed next to Mihai. Her warm body, from which the steam of the bath still gave off fragrant aromas, clung hungrily to Mihai's body, caressing his neck, chest, stomach, and his frozen thighs. Her bare breasts slid up and down his skin like pillows crushed under the fire of kisses while her hands desperately sought to discover some small physical invigoration that Mihai's body refused to show. They fell asleep chained like this, one and the other, or maybe they gave the impression that they slept, because the pillow on which Sanda rested was wet with tears.

After that night, Sanda never came down to sit in Mihai's bed. Grieg continued to come every morning and, together with Sanda, helped Mihai get out of bed, get dressed, and eat. Then, they would go together to their little antique shop on Harbor Front. Sometimes Sanda and Grieg went together to do small shopping for the home, leaving Mihai alone to deal with potential customers who, if they would buy an item, could insert the money into a wooden box with an opening like piggy banks fixed on the attached stand on the handles of his wheelchair.

After a while traveling in his van, Mihai noticed that on the front seat, Sanda's hands touched Grieg's next to her, a kind of familiarity formed between them that did not exist before. Grieg's jokes had become less veiled; they had a double meaning, and to strengthen their effect, Grieg turned his head back towards Mihai, winking at him. The distance between their bodies on the front seat narrowed and became insignificant. Mihai would have liked to draw their attention, but he could not say anything. He didn't say anything even one evening when the wind was howling outside, bringing a flurry of snow. Grieg allowed himself to be persuaded by Sanda to sleep in the guest room upstairs. Then, because of this invitation, it repeated, becoming lately a regular fact for Grieg to live in Mihai's house. But considering his daily help to Mihai, this arrangement seemed to please everyone. However, something, a hidden mechanism sprang in Mihai's heart and made him feel that something was wrong. Like each day, other signs seemed to tell him that his honor and dignity, which never left him, were in danger of being lost. For some time, Mihai noted, Sanda's negligent appearances in the morning at breakfast in the presence of Grieg, in a robe that allowed others to see, more than necessary, the shapes of her rounded breasts, made him say:

"Maybe you should get a more decent robe," Mihai suggested to Sanda one morning.

"Come on, Mihai, what the hell? You think I haven't seen women before?" answered Grieg. "As far as Sanda is concerned, that really doesn't matter. Only if you consider me a stranger can you do it. I consider myself a brother to you."

"Yes, but also in the presence of a brother, she must be more decent," said Mihai.

There was silence. One evening, in front of the television, Grieg opened a bottle of wine and filled three glasses. Mihai's glass, equipped with a straw so that he could sip by himself, was placed on a stand mounted on the support of the metal arms on his chair. Sanda was sitting comfortably on the wide couch in front, watching the movie. Grieg sat down next to her, glass in hand, familiarly cupping her shoulders with his free hand. Troubled Mihai watched silently throughout the evening, Grieg's hand resting on his wife's shoulders, surprised that she did not object in any way. Before the end of the movie, Mihai moved the wheelchair to his bedroom without saying anything.

"Mihai, wait until the movie ends, and we come to put you to bed," Sanda shouted after him.

<h1 style="text-align:center">4</h1>

When he woke up, Mihai was still on the chair. He was cold, even though he was dressed, and the sound of the television could be heard from the living room, which was still on. Mihai pushed the chair in that direction. The light was on, Grieg was lying across the sofa covered with a Scottish plaid, and on the top of the coffee table, carelessly left exposed, Sanda's blouse and bra from the previous day. Sanda was not there. It was still dark outside, and Mihai started to hit the stroller against the couch where Grieg was still sleeping soundly. When he woke up, he went up on one elbow, revealing a chest with sparse strands of bleached hair from under the blanket, and looking into Mihai's eyes, he said bluntly:

"Why are you staring at me like that? What do you think about me being a saint? After all, what do you believe I did wrong? Maybe I didn't seduce Sanda; maybe she seduced me... Come on?... But isn't she a human soul? Doesn't she have the right to be comforted? Better be a little more realistic! You can't satisfy her! This is the situation."

Mihai did not answer. He went back to his room, to the window where the morning twilight let in a little light. His consciousness was overwhelmed by the image of what he had seen and Grieg's words. What was he to do in this situation? He knew this was going to happen. Because of this, he tried to reject Sanda's words about marriage as much as he could, but in order not to make her suffer more after the sudden shock of the accident that turned the situation between them, he finally accepted. But now, what must he do?

"God, Holy God, help me! Inspire me! Teach me, what am I to do?"

Yes, what was there to do? In his situation, what options did he have but to accept the horrible reality that was formed without his consent? If he kicks Grieg out of the house, won't Sanda follow him? If he drives them both away, who will take care of him, who will help him every day, who will feed him, clothe him, wash him, put him to bed, and take him from there? He's alone! This is what Mihai achieved. He's terribly lonely! He chose this path himself when he left the country, relying only on his youth, on the health and vigor with which nature had endowed him, but in their absence now, loneliness brutally showed its hideous face by not letting him have any other option.

The first rays of the frigid sun outside produced sparks of falling frozen tears on Mihai's battered face. It wasn't long before Sanda appeared in his room, this time freshly wrapped in a house robe that covered her arched body. She lovingly approached Mihai's body and kissed him on the forehead:

"Forgive me, dear, the movie ended late last night, and you were already asleep in your chair, and we didn't want to wake you." she apologized, pushing the wheelchair towards the bathroom. "After we eat, if you want, because it's Sunday today, I'll take you to church because Father Silvan wants to see you."

Mihai did not answer. She washed his teeth and face, changed his shirt, Grieg knotted his tie around his neck, and they ate together, helped by Sanda, who divided the pieces from his plate to his lips. In his mind, meeting Father Silvan at the church seemed providential. He didn't know if he could confess, but maybe the saints in the icons would help him with an answer to his problem. In the church, the human soul is relieved, the silence floods him with peace, and pure thoughts take control of his whole being. If he doesn't find another option even there, he will have only one option left: death. After the service, Father Silvan stopped in front of Mihai and sat down on a bench in front of him:

"How are you doing, son?

"I don't know father... I wanted to ask you: are there facilities for people like me who can't move to be helped?"

Father Silvan looked at Mihai thoughtfully:

"There might be some, but I wouldn't advise you to go there. I once visited someone, and what I saw filled my soul with sorrow. But what happened?"

"No, nothing. I think that I am a burden, a heavy burden for those around me. They do everything for me, but it is not easy for me to receive their endless devotion. I would like to ease their burden."

"I understand... Why don't you go back to your people in the country?"

"Oh! Not! To them, I would be an even heavier burden."

"Yes, you are right... Give me time to think. I will pray for you son. Go with the Lord, and we'll see what we can do." said the priest, standing up, making the sign of the cross over Mihai's lowered forehead.

5

Lately, early signs of spring have flushed nature. The sun was coming up earlier in the morning, and its warmth seemed to be welcomed with joy by the new blades of grass sprouting from under the blanket of snow. In Mihai's soul, these signs brought more serenity after the discussion he had with Father Silvan at the church, waiting to receive news from him that would solve the dilemma he was in. Around him, after the discovery of the relationship between Grieg and Sanda, the atmosphere in the house became heavier, like an unbearable cloud that dominated the relationship between them. Grieg had started to become more aggressive, with bossy airs and subservient orders that irritated Sanda. She forced herself to endure his bouts of tyranny because she had not yet received the right to work in Canada and was forced to do what Grieg asked of her. They still went to their little antique shop together every morning, but Grieg would leave under various pretexts almost the whole day, leaving Sanda and Mihai to wait for him until he returned to bring them home. More recently, Mihai's car had a permanent stock of boxes full of beer bottles that were always being refreshed.

After that evening in front of the TV in the living room, Mihai never stayed with Sanda and Grieg to watch movies. He would go to his room by the window and ask Sanda to place a book for him on the stand that was easily assembled on the handles of his chair and read. Because he still couldn't move his hands to turn the pages of the book, Mihai used a stick that he took from a nearby glass with his teeth and helped himself with it. Often, he would sleep forgotten in his chair until the next morning when Sanda would appear to wash him and prepare him for the road. Grieg seemed less and less interested in participating in these activities:

"What me? Am I not doing enough for you? That without me, you'd both be starving by now."

As all the proceeds from the sale of the objects were owned by Grieg, when Sanda came to ask him for money to pay for some expenses of the house, whether it was the consumption of electricity, gas, water, or telephone, Grieg always objected that he was spending too much with them, that Mihai's house should be sold and find a cheaper apartment closer to the city.

"No more babbling!" he said. "What is the point of staying in such a big house when there is a lot of money here with which we can live like a king." Grieg would say.

One day, left alone in their small compartment with objects that seemed to interest no one, Sanda asked Mihai:

"What do you think about what Grieg said? Do you want to sell the house?"

"No. This property is the only thing I have left. If I lose it, I'm worth nothing."

"Yes, but don't you see how he treats us? I can't stand his antics anymore. If something doesn't change, I'll take my bag and head back to Hartford. Forgive me, Mihai, but I can't."

Mihai was not surprised to hear what Sanda said. On the contrary, he knew that sooner or later, this would be the outcome with Grieg, whom he never trusted too much. Even from his own stories, Mihai realized that Grieg lacked character and that his charitable actions from the beginning were just acts that hid his true face. After he seduced Sanda, the act became transparent, and nothing could mask his rudeness and true intentions.

"Do you think you can do what he does?" Mihai asked.

"What do you mean?"

"Don't you see that he brings things into his shop that no one buys? Could you acquire finer things and sell them without his help?"

"I don't know... I think so, but with what money?"

"Let's say I could take a loan from the bank and rent another space for our things... Didn't you see that there is an empty space next to the entrance now? It's even bigger than this."

"Mihai, you are a genius! How did you come up with all this?"

"I have moments too... How do we get Grieg out of our midst?"

"We tell him that you want to call the police if he doesn't leave on his own."

"Do you think this is how we solve the situation?"

"Well, what can he do? Does he'd run against the law?"

Indeed, when they got home that evening, before getting out of the car, Sanda told Grieg that he had to return to his house.

"But what, what happened?" he asked.

"Mihai doesn't want you to stay with us anymore. He said he's calling the police if you don't leave voluntarily."

"Well done! Really beautiful! After all I've done for you, you think that I am a burden, and this is how you repay me? I do remember that Romanian proverb about making someone good, is like stealing from your own mother. That's pretty much what's happening now. I didn't expect it from you, Mihai, boy! I'll go if you want, no problem." Then he asked Sanda: "Will you bring me to my home?"

"I'll bring you."

Left alone after Sanda went with Grieg to his house, Mihai could not imagine how simple this situation was resolved without much tragedy. He found it incredible that after months of suffering and torturous nightmares, Grieg agreed to leave them with a simple threat with the police. Anyway, from now on, another chapter in their life will start with the next day, and maybe it will be brighter and more trouble-free.

6

Sanda and Mihai went to the bank together the next morning. The clerk at the counter advised them that they had a better option, obtaining a line of credit with Mihai's property as collateral. With a lower interest rate, they could save significantly in comparison to a bank loan. The only problem is that to grant the credit line, the bank must assess the value of the property, which would take two or three days. After a brief consultation, they found the clerk's proposal justified, and they opened a line of credit in a joint account to which each had access. Their joy was never greater. They felt free from foreign influences and were confident in the success of their venture. In the meantime, they went to talk to the manager of the Harbor Front building and signed a one-year lease for the space on the first floor, closed to the main entrance. The advantage of this place was that most of the tourist buses had a stop there, and having the space close to the entrance gave them a prime chance to make their merchandise visible.

Mihai's property was valued at over two hundred thousand dollars, and the bank provided them with a loan of more than half of the entire amount. Mihai took out only twenty-five thousand at the beginning, enough to cover the first expenses. Since the money was put into a joint account, both he and Sanda had unlimited access to it, especially her, because she would be the one to purchase the new items and pay the bills. At first, on weekends, they would drive together through the wealthy neighborhoods where certain garage sales were advertised, and Sanda would pick out with sharp eyes what she thought would sell easily. She came victoriously with one object at a time to the car and showed Mihai what she found for almost nothing because she managed to pay only half of the requested price. Full of joy, they moved on, and soon, they had a collection of valuable objects with which they could open their new shop. When Grieg stopped by after the opening, he was amazed to see all these objects displayed on rented tables or hung on the walls, silk carpets, art reproductions, or even original oil paintings.

"Bravo! Now we are competitors, as I see...You took advantage of me, since you copied everything I did." Grieg commented, inspecting the objects.

Mihai found no reason to answer him, but Sanda asked him:

"Were we good students?"

"I'll give you seven out of ten mark" answered Grieg. "But where did you get the money for all this?"

"From the bank. I borrowed."

"Bravo to you! Good luck!" and left.

As the first busload of tourists stopped in front of the building, the objects chosen by Sanda proved to be appreciated by buyers who often fought over the same object. Other times, Mihai was caught alone in front of a group of customers who came when Sanda was not there, and surprisingly, even to him, he was able to answer each customer, negotiate prices, sell, and receive the due amounts. No one could experience greater joy than his. He never confessed to anyone, for these small successes fueled his soul with much optimism that still, in his undesirable situation, he could be useful. His need to get away from the vegetative state Fate had reserved for him, brought great consolation to any small sign of improvement.

Seeing that Mihai could handle himself, Sanda began to leave him alone, sometime knowing the usual hours of the arrival of the tourist buses, looking for merchandise displayed for sale elsewhere. When she saw a contains sale advertised somewhere, on which a whole house would be auctioned, Sanda would be the first among the buyers in such an operation. Happily, she would return with the van half-full of new items. At Mihai's insistence, their prices were more competitive than others, and souvenir hunters found good quality items to buy with reasonable price from a tour of their small store. Almost everyone found something to their taste and possibilities. Interestingly thing, even renowned stars from theaters and movies passing through Toronto came to investigate the quality, beauty, and authenticity of certain objects discovered in this precious treasure trove of rare pieces. Everyone left satisfied with what they found for their private collections, of which they were proud.

These were the most beautiful days experienced by Mihai after the tragic accident near Syracuse. The success of their venture began to be felt by both, not only in that soulful contentment that normally comes after passing through a destructive storm but also in fullness because, from now on, they were freed from the problems of money and unpaid debts. All this disappeared like a miracle. They earned enough to cover all the expenses, and they started to afford to exchange old things in the house for new ones. What made Sanda very happy was that she could now afford to buy fashionable shoes, dresses, and accessories. Sometimes, they would go out to see a play together, taking seats ahead of time in a box where Mihai was put in his wheelchair with the help of ushers in the hall. Who could have imagined that all these pleasures would be possible for him after the Syracuse episode?

Grieg wasn't doing too badly, either. It seemed that despite the economic crisis that many people were complaining about, their business with objects from the past was doing very well. In addition to the fact that Grieg bought a new car for himself, a real spacious limousine with padded leather seats, he started to wear elegant, expensive clothes tailored to him. All this showed that his business had improved too. From time to time, he would let be seen his misguided traces of character, but in general, he behaved civilly without showing anger after his expulsion from Mihai's house. They continued to be friends.

On the feast of Saint Michael and Gabriel, on Michael's name day, Grieg came bringing a bottle of champagne. They dined together, ate, and drank, and as an interesting program was announced on television, he stayed for the show. This time, even though he sat next to Sanda, he no longer wrapped his arm around her shoulders. At the end of the program, he said goodbye and went to his house.

7

In October, it seemed that a cold had left Mihai bedridden with chills and a high fever. It was a most inconvenient day for such an event because a shipment of items bought by Sanda at an auction was due to arrive that morning at their shop in Harbour Front. Someone needed to be there without fail, and Sanda had to go alone, leaving Mihai in his wheelchair wrapped in blankets to keep from getting worse. Shivering after the two aspirin Sanda had given him before she left, poor Mihai dozed off in his chair, his eyes closed, feeling as though everything—the house and all its contents—spun around him like a carousel that kept turning faster and faster, with him at its center. When he reopened his eyes after a while, heavy beads of sweat were dripping from his forehead into his eyes, making their way down his cheeks toward his chin. But the chills had subsided, and now he felt a bit better. The salt from his sweat irritated his eyes, and he started pushing his wheelchair toward the bathroom, where plush towels hung on the wall rack, wanting to wipe his forehead with them. Somewhat calmed after this, he left the bathroom and stopped in front of the table where Sanda did her bookkeeping, which was cluttered with bills, receipts, and various papers she had to handle.

On one corner of the table lay the bank statement for the previous month. Since he hadn't seen it before, he looked at the credit account he had opened when he decided to go into business with Sanda. What he saw on that paper terrified him: he remembered only withdrawing twenty-five thousand dollars from that account once. Now, the bank debt had suddenly soared to over sixty thousand.

"How did this happen? Did Sanda withdraw money from the account without telling me?"

New beads of sweat formed on his forehead, but this time, he ignored them. He couldn't believe his eyes that such a thing was possible. He had trusted Sanda. He understood that her past involvement with Grieg was a mere lapse he tried to forget, but he never imagined she could commit such an act, spending money without his consent, money that didn't belong to her. What was he to do now? How could he restore the money to the account to avoid losing the house, the only thing he had left, which meant more to him than life itself? This, his house was his only substitute for his lost backbone, the tangible proof of his accomplishments before the accident, and the support of his self-respect that hated dependency on others. But now, everything he got, all the items in their shop were worth no more than a few thousand dollars, far too little to cover the amount borrowed from the bank. The rest, where did it go? Sanda's outfits, her shoes, and the fine lingerie she recently bought might add up to a few more thousand dollars... But where did the rest go?

"Oh, dear God, forgive me for doubting! This can't be true... The limousine Grieg drives now must be worth at least twenty thousand... His tailored suits, the lunches at fancy restaurants, the airs of nobility he puts on, where did he get the money for all that? Could he have had access to his money too?" Mihai felt dizzy. "Sanda! Her connection with Grieg has continued all this time! I've been blinded by her sweet words and her care, and I didn't see that, behind my back, Grieg and she were conspiring to ruin me. Her hasty departures under the pretext of a new collection going up for auction, were they genuine? Or they were just excuses to spend a few quiet hours with Grieg in a hotel, paid for from my account? It was all a ruse, a facade, a diabolical plan they wove together, and I was their victim, their laughingstock, the fool whose misery they so carefully concealed..."

Mihai moved away from Sanda's desk, heading for the front door. Outside, a gentle autumn rain was falling, destined to last on this land for some time. Chilled to the bone, the autumn's tears trickled into his veins without bringing a single tear to his dry eyes. He didn't know the time, but he knew Sanda was due back soon. What could he say to her? Now that he had understood what no one else had told him, words were useless, like lamenting at the head of someone already dead. Oh, if only he were whole, none of this would have happened! But even if he had found himself in such a situation, he would have known what to do. Now, though?... The plan he had formed during his darkest moments of despair, after the tragedy in Syracuse when he realized he was utterly incapacitated, came back to mind. Now, that was all he could do.

8

Finally, Mihai saw his van pulling into the paved driveway in front of the house. Sanda got out of the driver's seat and opened the back doors to unload a few plastic bags. The drizzle continued, and she pulled up the hood of her coat bearing the initials of Coco Chanel to keep her hairdo intact. As she opened the door to enter the house, Mihai blocked it with his wheelchair, preventing it from closing.

"What's going on with you? Where do you think you're going? Can't you see its raining?"

"What does the rain matter?"

"Come inside and see what I've done today..."

"I've seen, Sanda. I've seen everything you've done!"

"What are you talking about?" she asked, puzzled.

"The bank account! You've ruined everything we've built! You've driven me to the brink and robbed me of the last shreds of decency I had left. That's what I've seen!"

"I robbed you?" Sanda snapped at Mihai, feeling the blood rush to her head. "I served you like a slave for a year and a half, and now you're telling me I robbed you? You made me pity you, you dragged me into this pit, you stole the best years of my youth, and now you're telling me I robbed you? Because of you..."

Mihai didn't stay to hear her out. He went out along the side slope of the stairs by the wall, letting his wheelchair roll down on its own until it reached the bottom, where the path was bordered by a low concrete step separating it from the green lawn surrounding the house. The footrest struck this edge hard, bending the chrome tube that held his feet, but he felt no pain. He followed the path to the street, ignoring any traffic heading his way. Sanda stood in the open doorway, her hand to her mouth, unsure what to think. Then, snapping out of it, she placed the bags on a table and hurried to the top of the stairs to see where Mihai was going. He was already on the opposite sidewalk, turning onto a side street leading to Kingston Road toward the Scarborough Bluffs. Panicked, she rushed down the stairs, got behind the wheel, and drove off in pursuit.

"What is this fool trying to do?" Sanda muttered to herself. "He needs to be stopped! In this rain, he'll catch pneumonia..."

Crossing the busy road with cars speeding by from both directions, Mihai managed to enter Guild Street, heading for the familiar park where he had once worked on restoring the building inside. Someone had saved the relics of old buildings from Toronto's center that had been demolished over the years: marble columns, classical pediments, vine-covered portals, bas-reliefs, and capitals, bringing them here to adorn a place that once served as an artist colony. At the edge of the park, a steep drop of nearly ten meters separated the vast garden and its ancient trees from the turbulent waters of Lake Ontario below.

Here, in his grief and despair, Mihai was rushing to reach.

This time, he was determined. His ties to the world around him had long been severed; there was no one for whom he could do anything, and no one who would shed a tear for him. He no longer felt like a person, more like he became an object—an obstacle in the way of others. Better off gone!

Pushing the rain-soaked wheels of his chair, with mud sticking to them from the path, the skin on his palms tore, exposing raw, bleeding flesh that sent sharp stings through him at every touch. It wasn't far now, and there, all his pain would end. He entered the park, advancing along the cobblestone path, feeling the rain cooling his feverish body.

"Just a bit more," he told himself, pushing his chair up the path. "Just a little further!"

He was almost there, the last few dozen steps between old trees, where no one else walks, and there nothing could stop him from reaching the cliff's edge. The precipice was deep, its base littered with debris washed ashore by the lake's waves. He didn't want to look down. Better to turn his back to it, to face the sky—the sky that hid behind clouds as it met his fate... The sky would see him and mourn for him...

Turning his wheelchair, he saw Sanda running toward him, waving her arms frantically. It was too late. He was now at the cliff's edge, just a few inches away. A simple motion of his arms, a last look of the trees around, the final roll of well, and...

"The sky! How beautiful is the sky, shrouded in clouds like the veils women wear when mourning a lover. And they weep, just as the sky weeps now, as I soar in air like a bird..."

Startled by the commotion, a white albatross took off with a long cry, soaring into the depths of the sky.

The Surprise

I pulled the door shut behind me and headed to the car parked in front of the garage. It was dark and cool on this December midnight in Boca Raton. Climbing behind the wheel, I glanced worriedly at the gas gauge, which warned me that I only had about an eighth of gas left in the tank. Too bad I didn't fill up earlier when I went out for groceries.

I was rushing to leave before the kids returned, replaying everything that had gone wrong in my mind. I had set out on this journey with such joy, all the way from Toronto, intending to surprise them in a way no one expected, not even me since the idea had hit me out of nowhere, like a cold shower on an otherwise sunny day. And now, here I was, heading back after just one night in my son Călin's house.

As I left in the darkness, I stuffed my suitcase with clothes scattered randomly in the bedroom. The rest—things from the bathroom, my toothbrush, other essentials, and even my passport, I remembered—I didn't take with me. I left them somewhere in the darkness of the room I hurriedly abandoned, where my wife, Vera, was either sleeping or pretending to sleep. I was boiling with anger and unable to rest, so I decided it was better to leave. No, I couldn't stay there!

On the road, in the car, following the route on the GPS on my phone, I was looking for a gas station while calculating that I didn't have more than a hundred dollars and maybe some change in my pocket. There were still 2,500 kilometers separating me from home in Toronto. At this hour, in the city wrapped in the silence of the night, cars were rare on the streets. I suspected that soon I'd have to get on the highway, and I still hadn't found a gas station. What am I going to do, I thought, if I run out of gas in the middle of the night on the road? How will I know which exit has an open gas station? I kept driving forward, following the GPS's instructions, blinded by the flood of thoughts and my still-unbridled anger.

I never imagined that I would be treated without respect in Călin's house. This, after eight months of living apart, without seeing each other much, and with only the occasional phone call. I'd been away from home mostly because of my wife, not because of myself. After more than fifty years of marriage, Vera and I could no longer get along. I don't know what happened, but over time, the differences between us had grown. There were always objections, petty arguments, and disagreements out of nowhere, followed by long stretches of silence as if we were strangers. More recently, about two years ago, coming back from a movie, as I tried to overtake a car on the road, she snapped at me:

"Why don't you drive like a normal person?"

"I don't understand. What's your problem?"

"Didn't you see that guy on the left honk at you?"

"So what? I didn't cut him off," I said.

"Yes, you did. That's why he honked at you. I'm tired of seeing you zigzagging through traffic. You know, you're making me not want to get in the car with you anymore."

"Are you serious? He was a hundred meters behind. No one likes having a car in front of them."

She turned to me furiously:

"So, I'm the crazy one now? You drive like a maniac, and I'm the one at fault? After all the accidents I've had to cover for you. I said it before, and I'm saying it again: I'm done. I'm not getting in the car with you anymore."

"Fine, that's okay. Then don't."

That was it. This time, she meant it. She never got in the car with me again. Whenever we had to go somewhere together, we each took our own cars.

At that time, Gabi, our daughter, lived with her family in Ottawa, four hours away from us. Vera decided to visit her for a week. I hadn't seen her in a while either. I would have liked to go too, but we couldn't drive 400 kilometers in two separate cars. It didn't make sense. I couldn't convince Vera to go with me:

"If you want to come, get in my car, and I'll take you there."

"Fine, but on the way back, I'll drive," I told her.

"No, I'm not riding with you!"

She left on her own. I was upset. I wondered how long we could go on like this. The situation seemed both irreconcilable and ridiculous at the same time. As she was leaving, I told her:

"If you really go without me, remember this: when you come back, you won't find me at home! If you want to be alone, I'll leave you alone."

When she left, I didn't even come out to say goodbye. A few days later, I also left, but not to Gabi's place.

* * *

No gas station in sight. Like it or not, I entered the highway. It was a toll road, about 60 kilometers long, leading to the north-south I-95 interstate. Dark, with just two lanes in each direction, all I could see were the road markings or, rarely, the headlights of an oncoming vehicle. On the lit-up dashboard in front of the steering wheel, I watched nervously as the gas needle edged closer to the empty mark. At the same time, I imagined Călin's surprise when he came home at this hour and found my car missing from the driveway in front of the garage. But then, a more doubtful thought crossed my mind:

"Will he even notice that my car was gone?"

* * *

In Vera's absence, while she was away, I found a newspaper ad for a furnished room for rent in a basement. I moved there. All I took from home were a few changes of clothes and my work gear. I continued to work part-time at an office on a contract basis. The kids couldn't understand my attitude and seemed hurt that I'd left home. Both came up with solutions: taking two cars, using a taxi, but I could only accept one solution, returning to normal, which for me meant the way things used to be.

On June 15th, I had planned a vacation from the city, a two-week stay at a resort in Lethbridge, Alberta. That region is part of the mountain range at the border between British Columbia and Alberta, known as the Canadian Rockies. Visitors from all over go skiing or relax in places like Lake Louise, Banff, or Waterton. But now, given the situation with Vera refusing to travel with me, I was in an unprecedented dilemma. What was I to do? The reservation, made and paid for in advance, couldn't be canceled. Being exchanged in equal manner with our time-share resort in Florida, I knew I would get an apartment with two bedrooms, a living room, a kitchen, and other amenities, spacious enough for a family larger than just the two of us.

I tried to convince Gabi to come with me. We could drive in

my car, which was big enough for both our families. It wasn't possible. The school year wasn't over, and Aaron, her son, was in the middle of his exams. I then tried persuading Vera to fly to Calgary, and from there, we could drive together to the resort. She refused. Then I suggested she take a taxi from Calgary. Same answer.

Three days before the reservation date, I set off alone by car. I hate long drives by myself, but this wasn't just a long trip; it was an enormous one: 4,000 kilometers. Four long days of driving with few rare stops, all alone, with no one to talk to. Three nights spent mostly sleepless in cheap hotel rooms, eating whatever I could find at gas stations. Above all, the constant battle with sleep. The unrelenting sun kept blinding me through the car's windshield, stubbornly aligned with the straight road like strings stretched on a musical instrument, tormenting me for much of the day. But I arrived safely.

The resort, nestled at the bottom of a canyon in the heart of the city along the Old Man River, was of paradisiacal beauty. I spent two weeks there in hermit-like solitude, isolated in an apartment where a family of six could have lived comfortably. The nearby mountains, the landscapes, and the peace helped clear my thoughts, though the fact that there was no one to share the joy of the beauty around me took away much of the scenery's charm. After those two weeks ended, on my way back, with no fixed date to reach my destination, I was more relaxed and able to enjoy the view and beauty of the journey. The metallic domes of silos rounded off in the distance, looked like church spires shining in the sun. The fields stretched wide like those in the Romanian region of Bărăgan, transplanted to Saskatchewan and Manitoba, with occasional silhouettes of oil rigs pumping crude oil from the depths, reminding me of trips on the Bucharest-Braşov highway near the city of Câmpina.

Reaching Ontario, a strange noise seemed to break through the sound barrier of a symphony from the CD, my sole travel companion, playing in the car's console. I continued driving without music, trying to figure out the source of the noise. Growing suspicious, I pulled over and opened the hood. The engine was running smoothly without any suspicious sounds. I checked all around the car, but nothing. I got back on the road, navigating the winding stretches, but the same noise returned, accompanied by a slight vibration that I couldn't quite pinpoint. I slowed down a bit, thinking the issue might be with the transmission. I knew I still had a thousand kilometers to go, and here, between rocks and lakes, who would help me if it broke down? I kept going like this for another hundred kilometers.

Suddenly, coming out of a sharp, downhill curve, the vibration became unbearable. I stopped immediately. I went around the car and saw the front passenger-side tire was completely flat.

The rim was dented in several places, likely from hitting rocks when I veered off the pavement. There was no way I could change the spare tire on my own, so I called CAA, my roadside assistance company. It took some effort to get through to a dispatcher. I had to wait about two hours.

It was a Saturday evening, and I was in a deserted area. Rocks towered on both sides, cars roared past me, and the sky above was like a domed mirror reflecting the scorched earth under the naked sun. Luckily, I had a bottle of water in the car to ease the heat of one of those first sweltering days of July while waiting for the CAA with the engine turned off.

* * *

It seems that despite my love for driving, a hidden streak of bad luck follows me. Just like now, here on the highway in the dark, with my gas tank nearly empty. I decided to take the first exit and wait for dawn. A sign at the exit showed a gas station on the right. I found the station, but it was closed. I turned off the engine, reclined the seat, and tried to get some sleep. Around six in the morning, someone tapped on my window:

"Are you OK?"

It was either a cop or perhaps a security guard making the rounds, checking the businesses. I nodded, opening the door to step outside.

"I ran out of gas last night and pulled over here to continue my trip in the morning," I explained.

"Where are you headed?" he asked.

"Toronto, Canada," I replied.

"There's an all-night gas station about two miles down in that direction," he said, pointing. "This one here, ever since the owner died, might not open at all."

I thanked him and drove off toward the station he'd mentioned. It was still dark when I filled up the tank and secured a cup of hot coffee in the holder, ready to hit the highway again.

I knew the kids, coming home late last night, were probably still asleep. They likely hadn't even noticed that my car wasn't parked in front of the house. Vera, my wife, I imagined, would already be in the kitchen preparing breakfast. What on earth was going on in her mind and heart? How could she not be disturbed by the absurdity of this situation, especially now, at our age? I just don't understand.

* * *

I waited over two hours for the CAA mechanic to arrive. The spare tire, anchored beneath the car's chassis, was rusted and unusable. He said he'd have to tow me out of this remote spot to a garage. At that hour, Saturday night, not a single garage would still be open. The mechanic suggested leaving the car in the Canadian Tire parking lot in Sault Ste. Marie until morning and dropped me off at a nearby motel. From there, I could walk to the garage the next day.

While waiting, I realized that only a miracle had saved me from the brink of an accident on the steep road with sudden twists between the rocky cliffs of Mount Ogidaki, at whose base the waters of Lake Superior ceaselessly churned. My God! I had come so close to plunging into a ravine. If Vera had been with me, she'd surely have had a heart attack.

* * *

The traffic on Interstate I-95 was livelier at this hour. The sky in the east took on a reddish hue over the curtain of trees lining the road. With the cruise control set at 120 km per hour, alone on the wide, three-lane highway, my thoughts wandered back to the events of the previous evening and my sudden departure from Călin's house. Did I do the right thing by leaving? Did I react like that proverbial old woman who got angry with the village over nothing? After all, Elena, my daughter-in-law, had every right to clean her furniture at will in the house. What if she started with the chair I had been sitting on? Like any housewife, she cared about her furniture, which she chose with such care: white, upholstered in leather. There was no reason for her to ask for my permission. But…

that was the only chair she cleaned. All her attention focused on that chair alone, nothing else. I remember every movement, the way she looked at me while wiping the chair with a damp cloth. It wasn't so much that she was concerned with removing a stain or anything like that; she was demonstrating to me that the chair I had used must be sanitized. She made me understand that my place was not there. I read on her face the desire to hurt me, the urge to prove her superiority, to put me in my place.

What it hurt most was that my son, standing right there, witnessing the whole scene, didn't react at all. I'm sure he saw everything, but he chose to let it pass, avoiding a conflict with his wife. Nothing new in that.

* * *

I returned from Alberta with gifts for the kids. Even for my wife, I found something I knew she'd like—a cup and saucer made of the finest China porcelain from Queen Elizabeth's commemorative tea collection, celebrating her 60th year of reign. I would have bought the entire set, but it was too expensive, so I settled for just one cup and saucer. I would occasionally drop by the house to collect my mail, especially when I knew Vera was away at church, and I left the gifts there. She had more frequent contact with the children. I never knew how to maintain phone conversations with anyone without a clear purpose, and even then, my calls were brief. Vera was different; she couldn't part from her phone. Everyone called her. Ever since I've been alone, no one called me. Nor did I call anyone.

I even went to Ottawa for a few days to visit Gabi, again timing my visit to when I knew Vera wouldn't be there. Another time, in the summer, when Gabi and her family came to Toronto to visit Călin, I went to see them, too. I sat in the shade by the edge of the pool, watching my children and grandchildren playing in the crystal-clear water through which the pool's bottom was visible. I admired them jumping from the diving board, under which a flat stream of water cascaded into the pool, or running in a game of tag both in and out of the water. It was such a beautiful day…

Increasingly, I began to feel loneliness and isolation from my family, from my children, and from all those acquaintances whom I didn't want to give the chance to gossip about our family. It didn't take long before I realized that word had gotten out anyway. The wife of a friend gave me a call. She insisted that I come over to see them. We set a date, and I went.

"How can you," she asked as we sat on the terrace of their house in the northern part of the city, "such a smart man, leave your own home, the house you worked for all your life, and go off with nothing to your name?"

For hours, over dinner and afterward, the conversation

revolved around the same topic, but there were no conclusions.

* * *

The highway stretched straight like a ribbon unrolling over sandy expanses, bordered by rows of straight trees like a curtain hiding the towns we passed, towns announced by numerous bright billboards along the edges. There were exits, overpasses, and bridges I passed under, occasional lakes or marshes, and groves of palm and banana trees here and there. The sun glittered on the mirrored surfaces of the cars that sped by. Călin called me a couple of times, but I didn't pick up. I stopped at a gas station to stretch my legs and grab a snack, a coffee, and some more water.

I resumed driving, setting the cruise control to the maximum speed limit, aiming to stop for the night somewhere halfway to Toronto, now about 2,000 km away. It was past 10 in the morning. To my right appeared the exit to Kissimmee, a town near Orlando where Walt Disney had established his famous theme parks. I continued north on I-95.

In Kissimmee, many years ago, I had bought two weeks of vacation time at a resort by a quiet lake. That was during our first vacation in Florida when we purchased our first week there. In fact, it was our first vacation outside of Canada. I think it was around 1981, though I'm not sure. I had already been working for a few years at the same factory as Ştefan, the head electrician, a fellow from Timișoara who had come here around the same time we did. He told me about what he had seen at Disney the summer before. Listening to his stories, which seemed unbelievable, I still believed him because I knew Ștefan to be a serious man.

So, for our next holiday, we booked a cheaper hotel in Clermont and headed there with the kids. We rented a car at the Orlando airport. It was July, hot, and our hotel was a 45-minute drive from Magic Kingdom. We spent the first day around the hotel's swimming pool. Back then, Călin was 15, and Gabi was 13. They were so full of life, always teasing each other.

We pored over a map we found at the hotel, looking for the quickest route to Disneyland. When we arrived the next morning, we were directed to our parking spot. Soon, we realized that Magic Kingdom wasn't just fun; it was more like exhausting work. It was impossible to experience all the surprises in a single day, with something remarkable at every turn, at every entrance surrounded by zig-zag queues of people waiting to take their turn at the wonders inside. In the tropical heat, the wait stretched to 10-15 minutes, but the anticipation made it worth the effort, the standing in line, and the swift passage of time.

As evening fell and the day ended, we returned to the parking lot, only to realize that I couldn't find the car keys. The enormous parking lot was packed with cars, but the kids remembered that we had parked in the section named Sleepy, the dwarf from Snow White. When we got there, we discovered the keys were not in the ignition, where I thought I'd left them in my rush of excitement. What to do now? I went back to the ticket counter:

"When did you arrive?" they asked.

"At around nine fifteen," I replied.

"What's the registration number of the car?" they inquired.

"Hold on, let me check," I said, rummaging through the car rental documents.

"Here you go," they said, pulling the keys from a nearby board.

Fantastic, I thought. It was hard to imagine a better organization. Just a kilometer away from the exit, on the road back to our hotel, we saw a big board which advertised a Time Share office. We didn't know what it meant, but we decided to check it out the next day. The kids in the back seat were already making plans for the next day. They wanted to go to Epcot, the new amusement park that had just opened that year. That day had been so amazing that we all kept reliving the incredible things we'd seen. We could hardly find words to express our awe at the technological advances displayed in the rides, games, and fairy tales brought to life around us, using flawlessly functioning mechanisms. The kids listed their favorites, commenting endlessly.

Early the next day, eager to be among the first at Disney, we drove past the Time Share billboard again and decided to stop. We found that we could buy a week at a resort during the kids' vacation period, with payments spread over two years without interest, at a price far lower per day than our current hotel costs. And it wasn't just a room; it was a fully furnished apartment with a kitchen, two bedrooms, a bathroom, color TVs, and all the amenities. This apartment could be exchanged for a similar one anywhere in the world. We thought it was a great deal and signed the contract without hesitation. Vera and the kids were thrilled that from then on, they could come here every year.

* * *

Entering Georgia after passing Savannah, I was trying to recall the shortcut to Columbia, as the GPS was only showing the fastest highways. This much shorter route led through a series of small towns where the speed was limited to 50 Km/h in town and a maximum of 90 outside. The truth is, I received quite a few painful fines for breaking the local speed limits in these areas, and Vera never missed an opportunity to remind me of them. Though the route was shorter, it still took at least two hours. Even if I continued south on the highway to reach I-26, I wouldn't have gotten there any faster.

This time, Gabi called me from Ottawa. That means Călin

must have reached out to her, saying he didn't know what had happened to me. There's no doubt they were worried, but I didn't intend to give them the chance to tell me that I acted childishly. No, they must understand that this was not a whim that could be forgotten. They needed to understand that I was upset for very solid reasons, not just for now but from before as well. I was angry at each of them for not making any effort to understand me, for siding with their mother every time Vera and I had a disagreement. Although I have no doubt that they both loved me, this constant solidarity with Vera bothered me. Even now, they're worried, but neither of them would admit that I was right.

* * *

After last night's incident with Elena, left alone in the living room since Vera had already gone to bed and Călin and his wife had gone who knows where, I started scrolling through the day's news on my laptop. I was staring at the screen from a distance, not understanding a thing, as if it were in a foreign language. I wouldn't have been able to erase from my memory Elena's fixed gaze on me, that treacherous, probing smile of my daughter-in-law, watching my reaction when she wiped the chair where I had just sat. There was nothing to wipe on that chair, but she cleaned it as if after a leper. Her eyes, the look she gave me, shocked me. Why? Was it because I had intruded uninvited into their lives, their paradise, or simply because I am different, an Israelit, a Jew? All the others are different, including Călin and Gabi. Their mother is Christian. They have something clean, something pure, but I am a Jew, thus dirty, "A dirty Jew" in the international connotation. A mere look, a gesture, but what a miserable humiliation!

How many times in my life have I not been treated to similar looks? Since childhood, at morning prayers at the neighbourhood primary school, where I was the only Jewish child in the entire class. Not crossing myself as everyone did at the end of the prayer, I became a subject of persecution by my colleagues. Even playing with other children on the street, I saw how they favoured me less than other boys for the same reason. Yes, I always felt treated differently than everyone else when I happened to be in the middle of a group, but alone with one of them, we had a good relationship, like there were no differences between Christians and Jews.

How many eyes have probed me in the same way? Certainly, many have faded into the fog of time, but some cannot be forgotten. They remain etched deep in my memory, like that moment when I was just a child and was horrified by the painful silence of my father as he held my hand, tears streaming down his face. The look and the brutality of the man who was yelling at us, pushing us down the steps onto the street. Yes, there were times and events that cannot be forgotten:

We were walking hand in hand, my father and I, crossing

over to Mr. Pârvu's butcher shop. It was a gloomy Sunday, and even the white walls of the houses seemed darkened, colorless. Few neighbors were out on the street, and a single carriage stood waiting for customers near the street corner. Many shop windows were plastered with strips of paper marked with the word "JIDOV" (JEW), diagonally covering the display of goods meant to attract buyers. A week ago, the postman had brought a telegram that grandmother was bedridden, sick for several days. Father, now jobless due to the law that prohibits Jews from working in enterprises with government contracts, stood bewildered in the middle of our dirt-floored kitchen, not knowing how to get to Pitești to care for his mother. I saw my mother bring out her jewelry in a handkerchief: her gold watch, a wedding gift, the bracelet gifted by my father, and a few rings, handing them to him. Father initially refused her offer, then, urged by her insistence, crossed the street to Mr. Pârvu's butcher shop.

Mr. Pârvu, a man in his fifties with a graying mustache, a young wife, and a little daughter of about five, agreed to buy the jewelry for 1000 lei but only handed over 200, claiming he didn't have more now. The rest was to come in a week. But that wasn't enough. Father then went to the bar owner next door to us, and Mr. Petrică loaned him another 200 until he could collect the rest from Mr. Pârvu. With these funds, Father rushed to Pitești to his mother to have money for a doctor and medication. But he arrived too late.

Grandmother had passed away, and the money now went towards the burial and settling other debts. When he returned home, the dentist in our courtyard was taken by the Legionnaires and beaten, forced to reveal where he hid his gold. He used to craft gold crowns for his clients, but all they found in his home were a few sheets of gold leaf as thin as paper, used for making dental fillings.

On that Sunday as we entered the butcher shop, there was a lady customer waiting to be served. After she left, Mr. Pârvu turned to my father:

"How can I help you?"

My father replied with a half-smile,

"This is a good joke. I came for the rest of the money."

"What money? I already paid you!"

"You gave me 200 lei and said you'd give me the rest today."

"The rest, you say. Wait a moment."

He went to the door, opened it, and called out to the street guard passing by: "Mr. Officer! Mr. Officer, please come inside!"

The street sergeant entered, and the butcher closed the door behind him. Mr. Pârvu shook hands with the officer and said, looking him in the eye,

"I have a nice tenderloin for your wife; she'll be pleased. But here's the thing: this man here claims I owe him some money..."

"And you don't owe him anything?"

"Of course not! Do you know me as someone who does business on credit?"

Mr. Pârvu's gaze shifted from the sergeant to my father, eager to see the impact of his words. The officer turned to my father:

"Is it true what he's saying?"

My father, with eyes brimming with tears, tried to find his words:

"Listen to me. My poor mother fell ill, bedridden. She died; God rest her soul! I had to rush to Pitești, and I had no money. I brought my wife's jewelry and asked Mr. Pârvu to buy them for 1000 lei. He gave me 200 because he had no more at the time and said he'd pay the rest today."

"Well, he says he doesn't owe you anything that he already paid."

"He only gave me 200."

"So, you did give him 200 lei?" the sergeant asked Mr. Pârvu.

"Yes, but that was because I'm a generous man. They weren't worth that much."

"But he says you were supposed to give him 1000?"

Mr. Pârvu stepped out from behind the counter, getting closer to my father:

"Listen here, you Jew! Do you think you can fool me? You come to this country to suck our blood? Get out of here, you dirty Jew! Out! Get out, and don't let me catch you around here again!"

With his eyes wide with anger, he pushed us out and slammed the door behind us.

Standing on the sidewalk, flushed and sweaty, my father wiped his tears with his sleeve. He paused for a moment, holding my hand, and then we went to Mr. Petrică, the bar owner.

"I need some time; I don't have the money right now," Father said. Mr. Petrică, who had seen the scene from his bar window, looked understandingly at my father, then took two small glasses from the shelf behind and filled them with brandy:

"Alright, drink this to my health. Good luck! We'll talk later."

"In a week?"

"In a week."

A look like the one I had seen in Mr. Pârvu's shop, unforgettable, lingered stubbornly before my eyes, superimposed on the image of Elena wiping the chair where I had just sat.

* * *

In the bedroom, I told Vera the whole story about the chair. She marked her place in the book she was reading and looked at me with wide eyes.

"I don't believe it," she said after I finished telling her everything and shared my conclusions.

"I think you just imagined it. I can't conceive that she could be that mean."

"Neither can I," I said, "but at the same time, her attitude, every gesture, every expression on her face conveyed a desire to hurt me. Do you remember when they came back from the beach this morning? She locked herself in her bedroom and didn't come out until evening. Only Călin came in a few times to bring her something. Why didn't she come out? Was it because I was in her house? And when evening came, and she saw me in the living room, as soon as I left the chair I'd been sitting on, she quickly grabbed a tissue to disinfect it. Isn't that malicious?"

"Calm down. Go to sleep. You'll see in the morning that everything will be back to normal. It's not as bad as you think."

"I can't calm down. I don't think you can either. What do you want, for her to shout in my face that I don't belong here? It's pointless for you to tell me to relax—I just can't."

"What do you want to do? Come on. Do you want to split them up? Călin cares about her. He'll never listen to you. He listens to her. Don't you see that you're fighting a losing battle? Come on, let's go to bed. I'm tired."

She was right. I took my pajamas out of the suitcase and got into bed. Vera turned off the light.

* * *

Before entering Columbia, I stopped at a gas station. I was exhausted, having gone without sleep for a night, and I needed a sandwich and a fresh supply of coffee. I knew that from Statesville, South Carolina, I still had about 12 hours of driving left to reach home the next day, and I was determined to get there before nightfall. For safety, I bought a pack of snack bars and a bag of chips, which turned out to be too greasy, so I decided not to touch them. As we got closer to the big cities, the traffic on the road increased significantly, especially during rush hours when shifts were changing at the factories. Police patrols became more frequent, lurking in hidden spots under bridges. Whenever a motorist was speeding, they would chase after them with sirens blaring and lights flashing. On the I-77 highway cutting north through the mountains between Columbia and Statesville, many small towns lined up one after another, like suburbs of Columbia's industrial center. The reduced speed limits and police presence noticeably added to the traffic congestion.

* * *

The same congestion greeted me every morning on the Don Valley Parkway in Toronto in the early 1980s. Back then, we only had one car, and both Vera and I worked on the northern edge of the city—she at a hospital, and I at a car parts factory. Those were tough early years after an immigration journey that had been interrupted by an eight-month detention in a refugee camp in Greece while we awaited our visa for Canada. Our progress was slow at first, but still, it surpassed the conditions we had left behind in Romania.

I remember the traffic jams on the road. Because of them, we had to leave home an hour earlier. I would drop Vera off at the hospital and then continue my journey further north to the outskirts of the city, where I worked as a chief designer at the factory. On the way back, Vera had to take four buses to get home, which took up a lot of her time. Only occasionally could I pick her up from the hospital because of the never-ending technical problems occurring in the factory. These problems forced me to spend long hours beyond my regular schedule finding new solutions almost every day, and often on weekends. On the one hand, these extra hours brought the benefit of a substantial increase in salary. But at the same time, they harmed my relationship with the children, who, despite our efforts, were mostly left unsupervised at home until we returned.

Vera decided to take driving lessons, and that's when I bought her a used Pontiac from a friend. Now, she could manage on her own—going shopping, taking the kids to their piano lessons, and getting herself to work. But it wasn't an ideal solution. We needed to find a house closer to our jobs.

* * *

Statesville was close to the Virginia border, and since it was too early to stop there for the night, I decided to keep going. Whenever I traveled to our resort in Kissimmee, Florida, I always used this place as a landmark; located at mile 50 on the road, where there was a small Fairfax hotel next to a gas station and a neat restaurant on the opposite side. Over time, however, the hotel came under the management of some new owners who, in their rush to recoup their investment, neglected the upkeep of the place. The number of guests dwindled, and the signs of decay became evident.

As I approached Virginia, the terrain began to undulate. The coming evening and the nearby mountains were noticeable by the drop in temperature, and I started looking for a place to stop for the night. I was so tired that I didn't feel like eating, but the desire for a stiff drink led me to look for a restaurant for dinner. After the meal, back at the hotel, I briefly flipped through the news on TV, started watching a movie, and fell asleep in an armchair, my head resting on my chest until morning.

After breakfast at the hotel, I settled behind the wheel, wearing my leather jacket and gloves, just in case it was raining and cold outside, as I knew that I was going to an area where winter was present. Soon, upon crossing into West Virginia, the I-77 cuts through the mountains on winding roads with dangerous inclines, and now, just before Christmas, there was a chance to find them covered in snow. Two days earlier, when I drove through here toward Boca Raton, I was lucky; it was a sunny day, bright like all my hopes of bringing joy to Călin's household. If things didn't turn out that way, it wasn't my fault. Regrets, yes, but no guilt feelings.

* * *

I was driving in the dark on the wet road without using cruise control because in that area, there were sections with speed limits lower than 80 km/h due to intersections with traffic lights. I'd been fined there before, caught off guard by the sudden speed limit change. Now, having learned my lesson, I paid close attention to every road sign. Many heavy trucks with enormous trailers started moving in the early hours of the morning, and in places, they occupied two of the three lanes. Now, past Bluefield, the silhouette of the mountains on both sides of the road started to emerge in the darkness, making me glad that I'd passed through the twists and turns of the Beckley area in daylight. It's one of the most beautiful and dramatic stretches of the road, and each time, the thrill of seeing those massive rock formations on one side and the deep valley drop on the other gives me chills.

After descending the winding slopes near the base of these rocky giants, there's a shortcut exit to the I-79 highway, which winds through West Virginia, heading northeast to Pittsburgh, Pennsylvania. The towns nestled in the valleys below the road, picturesque and inviting, especially on sunnier days, appear from between the mountains like a warm welcome for a cup of coffee and a snack while a mechanic attends to the car's needs for the journey ahead.

Near Morgantown, a road branches off to the right, leading to Washington, D.C., the seat of the United States government, where the Capitol and the White House shine in the center, surrounded by all the other government buildings. I remember this road well. We took a trip here in a rented RV when my parents first came to visit us after we bought the house in northern Toronto. The trip was splendid in our RV, equipped with beds, a small lounge, a bathroom, and a tiny kitchen. It was one of the most beautiful moments spent with my parents and the rest of the family after a period of economic depression and fear that we wouldn't be able to meet our financial obligations after purchasing the house.

We had just entered a severe economic crisis, where no one could be sure they wouldn't receive a pink slip for layoff the next day. In our factory, out of nearly 200 workers, only about 30 were still engaged in operating a few machines. In my design office, I was the only one left, working at the drafting table and handling all the issues that arose in production. The company's stock prices had dropped to a value that discouraged anyone from buying. I think we hadn't yet fallen into that 1982 crisis when I completed the purchase of our long-desired house, but the signs were not promising. By the time we took possession of the house, the situation had worsened significantly; the government, trying to attract foreign investors, raised bank interest rates to locals, as tourists were given big discounts if they paid in U.S. dollars. The lost jobs and rampant unemployment created despair and panic in the population due to the crisis that engulfed the entire economy.

Burdened by a gigantic bank debt with a double-digit interest rate and a monthly payment that swallowed half of my salary, I faced not only objections but also Vera's strong opposition to the idea of selling one of the cars to reduce household expenses. Our salaries were still quite low, the number of orders from the factory had decreased, and with them, the extra income from overtime disappeared. The money that had given me the confidence to buy the house was gone, and the threat of layoff hung over us every day like the Sword of Damocles. I lived a recurring nightmare every night and every moment of the day. But things got slightly better by the following spring, and that's when my parents announced their intention to visit.

IN PURSUIT OF HAPPINESS

* * *

It was cold outside. At the last gas station, I had to put on my gloves and even my scarf. I did regret not bringing something for my head from home. Actually, the only headwear I owned was a leather hat, bought a long time ago, along with my jacket from Denier, a company specializing in fur and leather garments. The approach to Canada was evident by the biting cold, driven by the wind, cutting through all layers of my clothing. Now, I was entering Pittsburgh. From there, the road would head directly north to Lake Erie, where I'd change course to the east on I-90 towards Buffalo, New York.

* * *

When I think about it, our life resembles a road. I can't think of a better analogy. In fact, it's like a winding road with many twists and turns; sometimes, it goes up, sometimes it goes down, and just when you think you can relax for a moment, a sharp bend appears. Then another, and then another. That's how life is.

We got together out of love after two years of dating. She was still a student in her final year of nursing school. I was working, just like my father, as an offset printer. We had no house, no money, and no prospects. My diploma as a technician in agricultural machinery didn't offer me a position in Bucharest, the capital city. We got married anyway because the date was set in advance, but even after the wedding, we lived separately. Where could we go if we did not have a place to live in a city half destroyed after the war? About a month after our wedding, my mother gave us her bedroom because my father worked nights shift at the newspaper. Since she slept alone in the bedroom, and I used the couch in the living room, she decided to switch places. Eight months later, through a lucky circumstance, we found an apartment to share with another family. Meanwhile, I found a job as a technologist at Sămănătoarea (The Seeder), the agricultural machinery factory. Soon, the children were born and knowing they would grow up while we only had one room, we bought a condominium apartment from the state. Speaking of twists and turns, how many have there been so far? The twists and turns on the road of our journey never stopped coming.

In our new apartment, we rented a room to some young people because the mortgage was too high and hard to cover. By this time, overtime payments were prohibited by law, yet the obligation to work whenever required without pay, day or night, remained, and it was impossible to live on just a salary. I found a private project for someone who needed a machine like the one they already had to double their production. It was a cooperative, and I agreed with the manager to draw all necessary parts for manufacturing. I went there, made sketches and took measurements based on his machine, and after three months of arduous work, mostly at night, I went to deliver the drawings for the promised money. The man rejected the designs, claiming he wanted the actual machine, no papers. It was something unbelievable. I could not understand that a sane person living in a communist country could demand such an impossible task. As there was no justice for deals like this, and the citizens had no rights, I worked for nothing. The disappointment I felt, coupled with the increasing difficulty of supporting a family despite all our efforts, drove us to file for renunciation of our citizenship in order to leave the country.

Life's twists constantly toss you from one corner to another like a ball bouncing on the deck of a ship. Looks like we are made of tougher stuff than we initially thought. Otherwise, how could we endure all these twists of fate and sudden changes in circumstances that we must adapt to without resistance because our survival depends on them? Without children, perhaps it would have been easier, but their well-being forced us to shape our lives around the unforgiving molds of a time that cared little, if at all, about what we wanted. Under the relentless hammer blows, steel is hardening.

* * *

The clouds filtering the sunlight grew denser, floating threateningly closer to the treetops lining the road. As I approached Buffalo, traffic slowed, and thick snowflakes drifted gently through the air like a speckled curtain, making visibility nearly impenetrable. If I were lucky, my view wouldn't extend more than 20-25 meters ahead of the windshield. Simultaneously, a pressing personal need became more acute, and I started calculating where I might find a restroom nearby and how far away it was. Distance would not have been a problem in that unpopulated area if people had continued driving normally, but as the snow piled up, many drivers started slowing down out of caution, making it impossible to pass them.

Now, the heavy snow entirely blanketed the highway, the wind had died down, and the road was indistinguishable from the fields on either side. Drivers formed a long, slow-moving line of vehicles, inching forward. My urgency was pushing me, so I pulled out of the lane, trying to reach the front of the convoy faster, aiming for the gas station built like an overpass above the traffic lanes in both directions. Across the road, a police car had stopped on the roadside, trying to assist a driver who had ended up in the ditch. I was moving faster than the line of cars, driven by the urgency that kept me from sitting comfortably in the seat, gritting my teeth under pressure, and soon I found myself at the front of the queue. There was no one in front of me now. Behind me, the others were following the tracks I had made in the fresh snow, trying to keep up with my pace. But in this white expanse where nothing stood out, I had no idea which direction to steer the car without suddenly veering into a ditch hidden under the fluffy sheet of snow. At last, in the distance, as far as I could see, the outline of the gas station seemed to emerge like a bridge over the highway, and continuing in that direction, I climbed the side slope leading to it. I was saved.

* * *

The distance from here to the border with Canada, across the Niagara River, should not have taken more than 15-20 minutes under normal conditions. This time, it took well over an hour. Usually, I would stop to grab a bottle of vodka from the Duty-Free shop, but I wasn't in the mood for that now. My passport was left with the rest of my money and documents in the safety pouch I'd forgotten two nights ago at Călin's place in Boca Raton. How was I going to manage at customs? What if they didn't let me through? What would I do then?

When I reached the border officer who was waiting with an outstretched hand for my passport, I showed him my driver's license and credit card, saying,

"I forgot my passport with my wife in Boca Raton!"

"Why didn't you come with her?" he asked.

"We argued, and I came back alone," I replied.

"When did you cross the border there?" he continued.

"Two days ago," I said.

He kept holding my documents in his hand, looking me straight in the eye, then picked up the phone and called somewhere. I waited nervously.

"Where was the last time you were abroad?" he asked again.

"In China," I answered.

"What date did you return to the country?"

"December 2nd, last year."

"Alright, you can go through," he finally said.

I sighed in relief. Once past the border checkpoint on Queen Elizabeth Highway, the sun broke through the clouds again, allowing me to continue my journey to Toronto on a dry road without a trace of snow. This phenomenon is common in this part of the world, known as the "New York Snow Belt." Nature generously showers the southern shores of the Great Lakes and the St. Lawrence River with snow, while the northern shores barely show any signs of it.

Tonight, I would be home. Home? What home? Where is my home now? I wondered. Here, in this place where I am staying now, enjoying the owners' friendliness and their frequent invitations to join their gatherings, I lived mostly in the solitude of my room, accompanied only by my thoughts and YouTube programs on my laptop. My real home abandoned eight months earlier, even if I were to go back there, would offer me more space but the same loneliness since Vera had decided to stay in Boca Raton for the entire winter.

* * *

Heading toward Hamilton before crossing the bridge over Lake Ontario, I glanced at the bay to my left, where ships were anchored along the shore near the steel mills. How many times had I passed through these places during the early years when I worked at Aero-auto Engineering Group as a draftsman? That was my first job close to my profession after arriving in Canada. To be hired there, I had to prove my skill in drawing uniform capital letters, which is essential for technical project indication and for the list of components on the blueprint. I practiced for weeks on graph paper with a soft graphite pencil; the lead sharpened obliquely against a sheet of sandpaper to shape letters with thicker lines in certain directions.

After being hired, I was given a drafting table in an office with 15-18 other draftsmen bent over their desks. The agency received sketches of new gas turbines produced by Westinghouse Canada in Hamilton to be properly designed onto standard blueprints here in this office. Soon, since I had my own car, I was asked to drive to Westinghouse, to deliver the drawings and pick up new orders. One of these assignments involved creating a full-scale cross-section assembly drawing of a new steam turbine with all its internal details from previously drawn parts to this master assembly. This task was bestowed on me as someone else took over the daily deliveries to Hamilton. The head of the office was an engineer past retirement age.

The agency's owners were simple businesspeople with no technical knowledge, easily influenced and fearful. A group of young engineers, unsatisfied by low wages, banded together to start a new agency by themselves, threatening to take over Westinghouse's business. Under the threat of competition, the owners replaced the older engineer with one of the younger men. As I kept a neutral position on office politics, when I completed the turbine project, the new office manager thanked me but said my services were no longer needed.

Luckily, I had kept copies of the drawings I'd done, including the turbine assembly. At least now, I could prove I had Canadian experience.

* * *

I returned to where I started, the house where I had rented a room in the basement. When the owners saw me, they came curiously to ask what had happened. I quickly said that I'd forgotten to submit an urgent project file and had to come back. I don't know if they believed me, but I was glad they left me alone.

I don't remember how I slept that night because the two days on the road hadn't clarified any answer to the question, what should I do? Here in this basement, despite the kindness of the owners, I lived like a badger in its burrow. Both Gabi and Călin kept telling me to sell our house, split the money with Vera, and move into a decent apartment. That would mean a final separation, a divorce. But I didn't have such a thing in mind. Divorce from Vera would mean divorce from everything I'd tried to build my entire life: a family. I didn't want to end my days as a miserable old man with no one around me. That wasn't why I had rejected temptations that could pull me back or the seductive offers that could have lured even a saint. Then what was to be done? I woke up the next morning with that question. After having my coffee, I decided to call Gabi in Ottawa.

"What's going on? Where are you?" she asked.

"In Toronto. I came back last night."

"Why didn't you answer the phone? You drove us all crazy! We didn't know what was happening to you!" Gabi's voice conveyed an emotion so intense it was close to tears.

"I was upset. Very upset. I didn't know what to say. I still don't."

"What happened?"

I started telling her what led me to go there, the joy I felt at the thought of surprising them, that we would spend Christmas and the New Year together, and that we would return home together, happy as if waking from a bad dream. Then I described what I felt and how much Elena's attitude hurt me, not her words but the venom that shot from her eyes like Medusa from mythology. Finally, I let all the black blood pour out of my soul. I told Gabi I needed her help:

"Do you think you could come with your car and help me bring everything I have here back home?"

"Are you going back to Mom?"

"Yes. I don't want to stay here anymore."

"I don't know when I can come. Today is Christmas. I have to be at home with Alex and the kids. Alex's mom is also coming over today."

I had forgotten that today was Christmas Day. Vera's sister and her husband had made me promise I would come to their house today for dinner, but that was before I decided to go to Călin's. Now, I didn't know if Vera had told them what had happened. After talking to Gabi, I suddenly felt lighter. I didn't know if I was making the right decision, but my immediate plan to go back home seemed to clear up the whole situation. I had a plan, and I knew what I needed to do. And then Călin called. Gabi must have told them I was okay.

"Dad, what are you doing? Why did you leave us?"

"You know why. Mom told you why!"

"No, that's not right. Come back right away!"

"No! I'm not setting foot in your house again! Thank you, but I've had enough."

"Why not? Elena didn't mean anything bad. You just misunderstood. Here, talk to her. It was a mistake."

"I have nothing to say to her. I don't like how she treated me, and I don't like how she treats your mother. Is it normal that in your big fridge, your mother survives on leftovers? Can't you see what's happening in your house?"

Călin, taken by surprise, started to get angry at my words.

"That's not true. We took Mom to restaurants many times. She doesn't want to go. We always ask her what she needs, and she says she doesn't need anything. You came here to ruin our holiday. You've upset everyone, including Elena. Is this the Christmas you've given us? Ask Mom how happy you made her!" He hung up the phone.

What kind of children have I raised? I thought. Up until now, he'd never done something like that. Has he forgotten that I am his father? Doesn't he need me anymore? Have I become irrelevant in his life? I didn't know what to think anymore. But to give credit where it's due, others depend on him now. Many others—his employees, partners, and even his clients. I must admit he worked hard to build his company. Ever since college, together with a few colleagues, he founded this software company. They struggled, they had setbacks, and some people even took advantage of their naivety and stole equipment from them through fake orders. But eventually, they succeeded, and now his firm is one of the leading companies for programs they developed. The same goes for Gabi. They worked hard, studied, and supported themselves. Both he and Gabi matured and accomplished remarkable things far beyond what we achieved, both materially and socially. They built prosperous families, and now, in the autumn of our lives, we need to accept that it's not them who depend on us, but we who depend on them. And we are proud of their achievements.

I often wonder what credit we can claim for everything they have achieved. We certainly did everything possible: we guided them, created the opportunities they needed, and always encouraged them. But other parents did the same, and not all their children turned out as ours did. Why? What's the reason? Who knows?

A wheat stalk grows from a seed that sprouted from another wheat seed. Could it be the same with people? We gave everything we had to these children; we would have given them even our lives because they were ours to give. We didn't have much money, and we still don't. But Vera and I were resilient; we had strength, and we didn't let problems overwhelm us. Our children inherited these qualities just as we inherited them from our parents, who lived in the same way. More than that, if I think it over, we come from a lineage eternally oppressed by others. Many came with envy to plunder what we had. They kept us captive because of our lands, our pastures, our forests, and our crystal-clear rivers. They even tried to change our ancestral faith. They didn't succeed. That's why we always stood guard, with our hands clenched on the pitchfork with its sharp tines, just like in 1907.

More recently, we endured two devastating wars. We survived! We survived even when they came again to rob us of our goods, our faith, and our freedom. We survived because we had no choice. From this comes our resilience, a resilience unlike that of others who have not known as much suffering as we have. Our genes are tried and tempered in our millennia-long struggle for survival. Our merit? Perhaps we do have one: that of passing down to our children the resilience accumulated over generations in our genes. Every molecule in our blood carries the message of the past, transmitted to our children's blood with an added dose of new, creative energy.

* * *

Not long after, Vera's sister called me. She found out I had returned and renewed her invitation to dinner. I went to their place and told them I would be going back home, and they were glad to hear it. That evening, I received a call from Gabi saying that they would come on Thursday, in two days, to help me with the move. Back in May, when I left home, I took only a few things with me, convinced that Vera would soon change her mind and we would return to normal. It didn't happen that way. What I thought would be a temporary move turned out to be long-term. So, each time I visited home, I started bringing more items to my new place: my computer, printer, and a lot of books and documents besides the things I had to buy because I didn't want to abuse the kindness of my landlords by borrowing what I needed. Now, to move back home, a single van wasn't enough to take everything back.

Gabi arrived on Thursday, a little before noon. I had everything packed for transport, but with her housekeeping experience, she managed to reduce the number of boxes and bundles that needed to be moved home. When she came here, she saw the room I had rented for the first time, and though she said nothing, I could read in her eyes the surprise that I had managed to live in such a cramped space. After we loaded everything into the cars with Alex's help, Gabi started cleaning the room I had used. Then, we left for home.

When we arrived home and parked the cars on the driveway in front of the garage, the front door opened, and Vera appeared on the doorstep:

"Welcome back!"

Emotion overwhelmed me, and I nearly dropped the box I was carrying.

"Good to see you, my dear. Good to see you! When did you come back?"

"Last night. Gabi and Alex came to pick me up from the airport. Călin and Elena are on their way. They're driving in tomorrow, so we can all celebrate New Year's together here."

"What are you saying?" Speechless for a moment, I turned to Gabi in disbelief. When I saw her nod, I said with a playful reproach:

"So, you knew all about this and didn't say a word?"

"Well, what can I say? You're not the only one who knows how to plan surprises!"

The Process of Shaping

The Interview

With the newspaper on his lap, Emil sat in front of the phone, hesitantly considering whether to call or not. For nearly a month, he'd been trying to get an interview for a job, but as soon as he spoke, he was told the position had already been filled. He had recently arrived in Canada with his family and had worked wherever he could find work, mostly unskilled jobs because his self-taught English lacked the persuasive power to convince anyone he was qualified for any trade. Now, fired from his last job at an agency that made drawings for various clients, he was desperate to find anything as the end of the month approached, and he didn't have money for rent. The hardest part was dialing the number. He felt overwhelming anxiety, even cramps. He feared that his stammering would bore people before he could explain what he wanted. Finally, he steeled himself and dialed the number.

"Hello, I read the ad in the paper," he said in English.

"Yes, you can speak with me. Can you come in for an interview today?"

"Sure! But I don't have your address," Emil said, almost intimidated by how smoothly the conversation was going.

"We're in the northern part of the city, in Concord, 232 Bow

Road. Not 'Lou,' it is spelled B as in Boston, O as in omelet, and double U as in whiskey. That's Bow Road. When you arrive, tell them you have an interview with Mr. Florescu."

"You said Florescu. Are you Romanian?" Emil asked, surprised.

"Yes! And you are, too?" Florescu replied, this time in Romanian.

"Yes, sir. My name is Emil Ciubaru. I'll come to see you as soon as I can."

"Good, I'll be expecting you."

Before leaving home, Emil looked up the address on a city map; it was on a small street just past the northern border, right below the edge of the printed map. He marked the spot with a pen and whispered a prayer for good luck. He then headed to the lift to retrieve his car from the apartment building's garage. He arrived in front of a massive, single-story red brick building at an intersection. Its façade revealed large windows encircling the building along two streets, with the entrance flanked by the emblem of a company affiliated with an international corporation. After asking for Mr. Florescu, the receptionist led him into a spacious office with several unused drafting boards. Mr. Florescu, a man about the same age as Emil, stood up from one of the tables and gestured for him to take a seat in front of his desk.

"Mr. Ciubaru? I'm pleased to meet you. Do you have a résumé?" Emil handed over his résumé, which Mr. Florescu skimmed quickly.

"Tell me, have you ever designed dies?"

"I must admit, no. I worked at Semănătoarea, a factory that makes agricultural machinery. From the ad, I understood that you need someone to do the detailed drawings. This will help me understand the dies and how it works."

"That's true, but it won't be easy for you. Here's the situation: Leave your résumé with me. You're the first candidate for this interview. The decision will be made by my boss, not by me, as there will be other candidates. I hope we get a chance to work together. I'll let you know what the situation is. Okay?"

Emil left feeling deflated. No luck again today. He came for nothing and used up half a tank of gas. He might as well have just mailed his résumé. Around him, on the same street in this industrial zone, a cluster of prominent company buildings made him feel a painful lump in his throat. How was it possible that out of so many businesses, there wasn't a single job for him? He was on the brink of tears, thinking he would return home empty-handed once again. A week later, Mr. Florescu called him.

"The assistant general manager, Mr. Mevison, wants to see you. Can you come here on Saturday morning at ten?"

"Of course, thank you!"

The manager's office was across from the receptionist, but on that day, she was absent, and Emil had to wait until someone passing by opened the main door for him. That same person went into the factory to let the manager know that Emil was waiting. Mr. Mevison was a robust man with a graying mustache dressed in a blue lab coat. He pointed Emil to a chair in front of his desk and began to read his two-page typed résumé. Emil's entire professional history, summarized in a few lines, was now being scrutinized by this workman-like figure with calloused hands. His expression revealed no hint of approval or disapproval.

"I see that in Canada, you've only worked as a draftsman in one place. How long were you there?"

"About seven months."

"Why only that long?"

"They told me they didn't need me anymore."

Emil felt humiliated admitting that he'd been dismissed by a new supervisor who didn't like him because the previous one preferred giving him certain tasks. But the story was too long to explain to the manager.

"Do you have any drawings you made yourself?"

"Certainly."

Emil pulled a folder of drawings from his briefcase and handed it over. Luckily, each drawing had his name written in the lower right corner box. The director, however, set the folder on the desk and left the room with a brief "excuse me." Alone, Emil wished he could take back his response about being let go from the previous company. Surely, it left a bad impression, no one is fired without reason, and he had no explanation to prove he wasn't at fault.

Nearly ten minutes later, the director returned and began examining some of the drawings from the folder.

"How did you know how to make these drawings? Did you copy them from others?"

"Some were derived from the project's assembly drawings. For others, I had the designer's sketches."

"And the dimensions? The tolerances?"

"I applied the standards of the company I worked for."

"Who checked them?"

"The company's engineers."

"Okay, I understand. I don't see any references here, and I don't understand why they let you go. While I'm gone, think about it and tell me who could give you a reference."

He left again. Alone, Emil began to worry, not knowing what he could possibly say when the manager returned. As for references, he genuinely didn't know anyone. In his forty-five years until he came to Canada, he'd never experienced what it meant to be fired. Wherever he worked, he'd done his duty conscientiously, and no one ever had cause to complain about him or his work. In Canada, however, things were different.

In his first job as a maintenance mechanic at a well-known hotel, he fixed and resolved many issues with installations that had been poorly repaired or neglected despite multiple complaints. When he was told there was a problem, he solved it to the best of his ability. When accused of insubordination and handed his dismissal notice, he was at a loss for words. In his next job at a luxury furniture factory, he was assigned a machine that simultaneously cut both sides of expensive, polished panels. Many of these panels were heavy, and since he had no one to help, Emil did the work of two people by himself. He didn't know that the other workers were in a dispute with management over this. When deeply scratched panels began to appear among those he cut, he knew the other workers were sabotaging his work. Soon after, he lost that job as well.

At the agency where he was employed as a technical draftsman, the old department head, an engineer past retirement age, was replaced by a younger man. The agency's owners, businessmen with no technical background, were blackmailed by a group of employees threatening to start their own agency, taking clients with them. Emil tried to stay neutral in this conflict but found himself among the unemployed once again.

"Did you think about it?" the director asked when he returned.

"I don't think I have anything to tell you. Just this: I had never been fired until I came to Canada. The truth is, I don't even know why I was fired. That's all. I don't know who could give me a reference."

"What salary do you expect to earn here?"

"I have no idea. That's for you to decide."

"Alright, that's not an issue. I want you to answer this: What guarantee do I have that if I hire you, you won't leave for another job that pays twenty cents more than we do?"

Saying this, Mr. Mevison left the office once more.

Emil felt the interview was a disaster, worse than any other he had attended. This man, the manager, didn't seem interested in talking to him seriously; he had more important things to do. Otherwise, why would he keep leaving the room? He felt like he'd wasted his time again. This time, he decided he had nothing to lose. Determined to end this situation, when Mr. Mevison re-entered the office, Emil moved in the middle of the doorway, signaling that no one would pass through without pushing him aside.

"You asked me what guarantee I can give you. You have in

front of you a certificate proving I worked eighteen years in the same company. The past, I admit, is no guarantee, but it's still an indication that a person is stable. Don't you agree? Do you think I didn't face challenges in those eighteen years? Do you know how many people resented me for insisting on doing things the right way, how many days and nights I lost fixing others' mistakes, or how many times I was threatened with dismissal for no reason? But I stayed. I kept doing my job even when I was offered better opportunities. I stayed because I didn't want the work I started to be finished by someone else, and because there I had many decent people around me."

Mr. Mevison, keeping the expressionless poker game face, watched Emil's plea from his chair without intervening.

"I'd like to add something," Emil continued. "In that thick folder with the drawings at the bottom, there is a full-scale assembly drawing of a steam turbine that I made. I worked at a factory that made agricultural machinery; they didn't make turbines there. However, I was given the task of making this drawing here using the technical details of the component parts."

Mr. Mevison unfolded the drawing.

"I've never done tool-making either," Emil went on, "but I know my trade, and I don't think you'll have any problems. That's all I can say." Emil returned to his chair while Mr. Mevison stood up, handed him the folder, and said:

"We'll let you know next week what we've decided." He shook Emil's hand and left for the factory floor. Emil packed his things into his briefcase and headed to his car. On the way, he lit a cigarette to calm his nerves. It wasn't until the following Friday, around noon, that Mr. Florescu called him.

"Congratulations! You can start working with us on Monday morning."

Marian

With a sleepless night behind him, Emil was driving through the traffic on the slick highway, blinded by the high beams of oncoming cars. He headed north, bypassing Highway 7, which marked the urban boundary. He was both excited and worried at the same time: a new job, new bosses, products he knew nothing about, and the uncertainty of whether he would be able to understand and meet the requirements of his new position. The unknown ahead of him was as dense as the early morning darkness outside, and he still didn't know what products the factory produced. Other than the fact that Mr. Florescu worked on designing dies, he knew nothing. Dies? What kind of dies? In the factory where he had worked in Romania, there was a toolmaking department that produced various dies for stamping sheet metal parts. Though he hadn't directly worked with those dies, he learned that there were many formulas, rules, and even many standardized products available commercially. Would it be the same here?

When he arrived at the parking lot of the building on Bow Road, Emil grabbed his briefcase with a sandwich that his wife, Coca, had prepared the night before, along with his drawing tools: B2 pencils, a compass, a protractor, and a set of squares of various angles and sizes. He thought once more to himself, "God help me!" and made his way toward the entrance of Rollform Manufacturing, where he would finally announce his presence on his first day at work. The receptionist, surrounded by a polished wooden counter near the entrance, examined Emil carefully with a curious gaze.

"Good morning!" Emil said in English. "I am Emil Ciubaru, the new employee in the design department."

"Mr. Florescu hasn't arrived yet. Please wait here until he does."

Emil noticed the few empty chairs in front of the receptionist and sat down on one. Meanwhile, many people entered in groups or individually, some hurrying past, ignoring the receptionist, and disappearing through the corridor to the right, where there was a brown door with a window. This corridor led to the office where he had been for his interview with Mr. Florescu. Directly in front of the receptionist, next to the entrance, was the office of the assistant general manager, Mr. Mevison, with whom he had his last interview.

To the left of the receptionist was another office with polished double doors, and the corridor extended perpendicular to the one he was sitting in. Some of the newcomers were heading in that direction.

A young, petite blonde woman dressed in black approached Emil as he waited.

"Are you Imail Shooberu, the new engineer?"

"I am E-mi-l Ciu-ba-ru." It wasn't the first time Emil had encountered difficulties with colleagues who mangled his name.

"Imil Shoobarru? Is that right?"

"Almost. E-mi-l sounds better."

This conversation took place as they walked down the corridor that ran perpendicular to the entrance, where the administrative offices were located.

"My name is Shandy, and I'm the office manager. I'll give you the employment form to fill out, and during the break, I'll ask you to go to the Bank of Nova Scotia on Highway 7 to open a personal account. Our salaries are automatically deposited there."

As she spoke, Shandy led Emil to her office, where she took off her coat and boots. Before sitting at her desk, she opened a cabinet and took out the form, handing it to Emil.

"Once you've filled it out, bring it back to me, okay Emil?"

He smiled and nodded.

Meanwhile, his new boss, Mr. Florescu, arrived, and when Emil saw the door to the office he had previously been in was open, he headed in that direction. When his new boss saw him enter, he greeted him with:

"Good morning," and added, "Mr. Ciubaru. Can I call you Emil? You can call me Marian. You know how it is with the English; they talk to everyone informally. It's simpler. I think you should sit at this drafting board so I can see what you do, and we can talk. Here's your workspace. What do you think?"

Saying this, Marian moved over to the drafting board closed to the door, equipped with a lamp on an adjustable arm with sliding plexiglass rulers. The desk in front of it was solid with two lateral drawer compartments. A long table between the desk and drawing board, like Marian's own place has, was to be used for spreading rolled-up drawings out. Behind these two aligned drafting boards, Emil's and his boss, were two other similar boards, each accompanied by desks of the same size and tables, but no one was working there. Marian's board was next to the window through which just raised sun above the rooftops outside, casts slanting rays of light into the room.

Curious, Emil glanced over the drawing spread on Marian's table but could only make out the outline of lines running parallel from the top to the bottom edge of the sheet. Catching his gaze, Marian returned to his place at the drafting board and explained:

"This drawing helps me calculate a pulley scaled at ten to one, meaning ten times larger. This way, I determine the technological process. You'll see that in this drawing you'll find most of the dimensions you need for the details you'll be working on."

"I understand, but at first glance, it looks like straight roads on winding paths... Excuse me, but I don't even know what product this factory produces."

"You're right. Let me give you a tour of the factory."

Emil followed Marian through the brown door with a window in the middle of the corridor. They passed through a short hallway with two closed doors and entered the main factory hall through another door with a glass pane. They found themselves in a vast, brightly lit space filled with neon lights, with tall presses nearly reaching the ceiling's support beams, lined up in rows stretching deep into the hall, alongside many other machines Emil couldn't identify. Ahead of them was a line of workbenches surrounded by lathes, drills, milling machines, grinders, and other equipment.

Marian led him straight to the workshop area near the lathes, where a short man with shiny black hair was surrounded by two others, all wearing blue overalls.

"This is the workshop foreman," Marian said, turning to Emil, "Amando, I'd like you to meet Emil, our new engineer who's starting today."

"Oh, great! Welcome to our team," said Amando, shaking Emil's hand. "Here's Vini; he runs the rolling section, and this is Vasile, the king of the lathe operators."

"Don't believe him," said Vasile modestly in Romanian, a slightly older man with a buzz cut and a round face. Emil shook hands with each of them.

"Good luck! Are you Romanian?" Vasile asked.

"Yes, nice to meet you."

"Another Romanian?" Amando asked in English.

"I was looking for an Italian but couldn't find one," Marian joked, exchanging a wink with Vasile. "Italians only know how to build houses."

"Houses that last a thousand years," retorted Amando.

"Who lives for a thousand years? Don't you see they're demolishing even the houses built just a generation ago to make way for new buildings? In Romania, there are houses over six hundred years old, but who wants to live in them? People want comfort, hot and cold water, baths, heating, swimming pools... New times, new lives," Marian said, leading Emil away from the group.

"Amando is a good guy; he knows his trade and is smart. We call him the Dwarf because he's short. He's Italian, just like Vinicio. But Vini is different; I think his mother must have made him with a telegraph pole. He thinks he's a prima donna because he was brought over from another pulley factory, and only he knows how to make them. We nicknamed him 'the Frog' because he's slimy; you'll see."

Marian guided Emil to the side of the building, where a row of vertical machines was lined up, placed at an angle to each other. In front of each machine, young women in blue overalls and thick cotton gloves were taking circular pieces from wide metal baskets and placing them on a device at the center of the machine. They would then press a button on a bar suspended by a movable cable. The upper part of the machine slid over the piece and began to spin rapidly while lateral arms supporting various rollers shaped grooves into the original piece. Once the task was completed, the supporting arms of the rollers retracted, the machine stopped spinning, and the pieces were released as the upper part withdrew. The worker placed the processed piece into another basket while retrieving a new piece from the original basket to install in the machine. Emil, absorbed by the process, felt as though the machine mimicked a potter's wheel, shaping clay into the imagined form of the artist, and he wished to witness the entire operation once more.

Called to another machine, Marian signaled for Emil to

follow him. There, two or three other people were gathered, and among them, Vinicio was having an animated discussion with Mr. Mevison, the manager. Emil stopped at a short distance from the group while Marian waited to see why he had been called. Mr. Mevison pulled him closer to show him a piece rolled with multiple, fine grooves resembling saw teeth. He seemed displeased with the piece he held in his hand. Vinicio had a metal template with teeth like those on the piece, which, when applied over the rolled grooves, didn't completely block the light from passing through.

Marian took the piece from the director's hand, examined it with Vinicio's template, and shrugged mockingly, saying that either the roller hadn't pressed deeply enough into the piece or there wasn't enough metal accumulated in the grooved area to fill the tips of each tooth. Saying this, he moved away from the group, while Vinicio, dissatisfied with Marian's comments, tried to convince the director that Marian was wrong:

"Everyone here has their opinions! I'm the only one who saw from the beginning that this piece couldn't be made, but no one believes me!"

Marian stopped Emil at a distance from the group and explained:

"The blond guy on the left is the general manager, Gerry, and the other one with the goatee is Konrad Boyden, his brother, who runs another company. They bought this factory about a year ago. It used to produce car pulleys, but it went bankrupt. They spent a fortune over eight years trying to create a new type of pulley, a poly-groove with many channels. This product is supposed to revolutionize the automotive industry because it can use a single drive belt for all engine accessories. Nobody knows how they intended to make them, but all the tools they used are here in our factory. Gerry, our director, and his brother want to continue what the previous owners couldn't achieve. Vini, that idiot has no clue what he's doing, always panics, messes with the setup, replaces the rollers, and then yells that it can't be done. It's laughable."

"Why did they call you?" asked Emil.

"I have nothing to do with them. I don't even need to. They come to me with a piece, tell me how to modify it, I make a drawing, give it for production, and then it's their problem. I don't get paid to do research or develop new technologies. Everyone sticks to their job because nobody else is going to do mine."

Saying this, they headed toward their office, where Emil still hadn't had a chance to arrange his things. Only now did he understand why Mr. Mevison kept leaving for the workshop every fifteen minutes during his interview. It seemed that the burden of developing the new product weighed heavily on his shoulders. Before sitting at his desk, Emil glanced once more at Marian's drafting board, trying to make sense of the lines on it:

"I get the feeling that what I'm looking is a V-shaped grove profile for a trapezoidal belt. Am I right? I remember that back home, pulleys like this were made of cast iron, and the belt groove was machined."

"Exactly. Do you realize how much lighter and cheaper this sheet-metal pulley is compared to the one in Romania? What we do here in minutes used to take a whole day there. See this drawing of the pulley?" He showed him a printed drawing on a sheet of paper. "The difference between this drawing and the one on the board is that you see it magnified ten times. Why? Because I need to calculate the exact size of the sheet metal needed for it. Do you understand?"

"I understand. But I also see other shapes in the 10:1 drawing."

"Those are the stages the initial sheet metal blank goes through until it becomes a pulley."

"Why so many stages? Can't it be done in just one?"

"No! The material would break. There are specific proportions for how much a blank can be plastically deformed in each stage, depending on the material's elasticity."

During this time, the workers in the factory had a brief 15-

minute coffee break, and the time clock bell near the tool shop signaled its end.

"Do you want a coffee? We have a cafeteria in the back. Come with me!" said Marian.

The cafeteria was a large room with tables and chairs like a restaurant, a free coffee machine for the workers, and two other vending machines where they could buy snack packs or soda. They each got a coffee in cardboard cups and headed back to their office. On the way, they passed by Amando's desk, which was situated near the wall in the corridor between the glass door leading to the factory and the room where Marian worked. Amando turned around in his chair and addressed Emil:

"How do you like it here?" Taken by surprise, Emil responded awkwardly:

"I don't know. It's interesting. Everything I see here keeps spinning in my head, like the rotating machines in the factory."

"That's how it is on the first day. You'll get used to it. It'll be OK, you'll see!"

"Thank you!"

Finally, Emil sat in his chair at the desk. Marian lit a cigarette and asked Emil if he smoked.

"I'm trying not to anymore. One less expense," Emil said.

"Back home, I used to smoke 8 Carpati, and it lasted me the whole day. Here, I have to buy a pack of 200."

"Do you have a family, kids?"

"Two. Nine and seven. They're in school. My wife, a nurse, works in instrument sterilization section at a hospital. She was lucky to get the job. How about you? Are you married?"

"I'm living with a girl. She's Romanian too. I found her here."

Emil placed the form he had received from Shandy on the desk. In the drawers, he found a pen, a few pencils, a notepad, and an ashtray.

"The office manager, Shandy, gave me this form to fill out. She said I should go to the bank on Highway 7 to open an account."

Marian didn't reply. Emil finished filling out the form and left to submit it.

Shandy

Shandy was alone in her office, which was cluttered with piles of papers, a typewriter, and, on the right, another electric calculating machine with a roll of paper. She was busy and didn't seem to notice that Emil had stopped in the doorway, watching her profile as she moved. To get her attention, he raised his hand to his mouth and coughed discreetly twice. She turned her head, and upon seeing him, she exclaimed:

"Oh, Emil, did you bring the form?"

He handed her the paper as he approached Shandy's desk, and she began to read it. Then, she told him to come with her to introduce him to the office staff. She knocked on the door of the office next to hers, and they entered:

"Norm, this is Emil, the new engineer. He started today."

"Welcome aboard," Norm said, standing up. "I handle supplies here. If you ever have any issues with the sheet metal we use or any other materials, come to me, and I'll be happy to help."

"Pleased to meet you," Emil replied, shaking his hand before they moved on.

Along the wide corridor, they passed two more offices where a girl named Patricia, and a young man named Paul were working. A side door with a glass panel revealed a room filled with workbenches equipped with tools. Next to the wall stood a machine slightly taller than a person, with a circular screen illuminated from within. Shandy mentioned that this was the technical control department and led him to a man with the beginnings of gray hair, Alex, who was engaged in a conversation with a tall, black-haired young man named John. Alex seemed to be reprimanding John, reminding Emil of some of his more abusive teachers. Shandy introduced Emil to both, ignoring the tension in the room. Then they moved to knock on the double doors of the general manager, Gerry Boyden and entered.

The room was spacious, with long curtains on the windows overlooking the two streets on the corner. The office was opulent, with two large, leather-upholstered armchairs and a matching sofa, all in harmony with the maroon color of the mahogany-paneled walls. Gerry was reviewing some data on sheets of paper, and when he saw Shandy, he called her over to his side behind the desk:

"Why are we sinking deeper into debt instead of cutting these expenses?" he asked while caressing her waist with his right hand, moving it gently up and down her back. Embarrassed, Shandy glanced at Emil, searching for a suitable response to the boss.

"It's January. December was slow. We had to cover bonuses, salary increases, and the Christmas party for the employees. We also gave gifts to our suppliers, clients, and certain important figures, so there was no way around it." She then turned to Emil, gesturing at him. "This is Emil Shoobarru. He just started with us and will be working with Marian in engineering."

"I saw you earlier in the factory, at the spinning section. We need to find a solution to get that pulley done. The company's future depends on it. So, we'll need your help. Be ready to see this through! If it means working day and night, we'll do it. Welcome aboard!"

After they left the director's office, Shandy stopped by the receptionist near the entrance.

"This is Megan. Emil started working with us today," Shandy said, introducing him.

When Shandy looked ready to head back to her office, Emil stopped her.

"One moment, please. I need to go to the bank. What should I show them? What should I say?"

"Nothing much. Just tell them you work here, and you want to open an account. They'll give you a booklet with your account number, and you'll hand that to me, and that's it! OK?" Emil smiled at her.

"Thank you, Shandy."

After lunch, Marian took a roll of calc papers from a compartmented box and spread them out in front of Emil. One large drawing, the size of the entire drafting board, was a 10:1. The set included assembly drawings of a stamping die and various other dies and devices. Emil felt a mix of unexplainable excitement and doubt but tried to keep his composure. He needed focus, some quiet, and a bit of time to decipher the intricate lines on the transparent tracing paper.

Marian pointed to the drawing Emil was to start with: a blank and draw die from the first stage. Careful not to ask questions before trying to understand on his own, Emil spread the drawing on his drafting board beneath the Plexiglass rulers of the drafting arm. He visualized the raw material entering the die, saw the massive lower piece of metal, the punch, rounded on top like a mushroom used for knitting socks, and noticed how the material was bent over it under the pressure of a ring with a rounded interior.

To confirm, he checked the 10:1 drawing to see if it matched what he saw in the die. It did. A quiet joy gave him hope that he was on the right track, that he could decipher the essential elements of this die on his own. Visualizing the top and bottom views of the die's open jaws in his mind helped him understand how this tool worked. It was like solving the mystery of an incomprehensible situation. Without a doubt, today was opening a new chapter in his life, like the promise of a good day at sunrise. "God, please help me!"

At precisely three o'clock, Marian put down his pencil, stowed the objects on his desk into drawers, and headed toward the office door to grab his coat and fur hat. Noticing Emil still working on a tracing paper spread out on his drafting board, Marian said:

"See you tomorrow then. Are you staying longer?"

"Just a bit more. Have a good evening!"

Marian nodded and left. Behind Emil, the door with the glass window to the corridor fluttered with the traffic of people coming and going at shift-change time. Emil wanted to stay alone for a while to deeply study the project before him. He had grasped the die's operating principle, how the strip of sheet metal was guided inside the tool, how it cut out the semi-finished shape of a blank, and how the cup was formed under the press's intense power. He noticed a pressure ring around the punch, actuated by four rods, and deduced that it was used to eject the formed piece, although he couldn't see where the pressure for these rods came from.

He inclined the drawing board to a convenient angle and spread the assembly drawing on it again. Each part was linked to a small circle with an identification number. In the drawing's right-hand corner, every number was described in the legend. Emil began following each one in sequence. At that moment, Shandy appeared at the door behind him, wearing her coat and ankle-covering boots.

"Hi, Emil. How's it going?" Emil, surprised, turned to her.

"Oh! Thanks. I think it's going well."

"I spoke to Gerry. I think you made a good impression on him. When I told him that Mr. Mevison offered you $5.75 an hour, he said to give you $6. I wanted to let you know."

Shandy wasn't beautiful. Small, blonde, wiry, and with crooked teeth that showed every time she spoke, she wasn't the kind to attract anyone, let alone men. But Emil wanted to hug and kiss her. Six dollars an hour was the highest wage he had received since arriving in Canada. At his previous job, before he was laid off, he was earning only $3.90. Shandy watched the effect of the surprise on his face, smiling. She wasn't conventionally pretty, but her energy, the way she moved, and especially the intelligence shining in her eyes made her more than attractive—she was a living target and a challenge for any man. And she knew it, using it to her advantage.

"When you leave, make sure to clock up. I already marked your starting time in ink," Shandy said from the doorway as she left.

"Thank you, Shandy."

"You're welcome."

After Shandy left, Emil found it hard to pick up the threads of his thoughts again. Starting at six dollars an hour was an unexpected blessing, and he felt the joy wanting to share this news with Coca, maybe celebrate it at home. As he was gathering his things from the desk, Amando, noticing the light in the engineering office, stepped in.

"You're still here?"

"Yes, I stayed a bit longer to study this die."

"If you don't understand something, you can always ask me. I know it's not easy to grasp everything on your first day, and I'd be happy to help you out."

This man, who seemed to be no older than 30-35 years, had a friendly face and a smile that drew you in. His dark, shiny hair, Mediterranean complexion, and sharp eyes made him an engaging presence, even though he was shorter than Emil by a hand's width.

"Yes, for example, this ring here," Emil pointed to the ring around the punch at the die's center. "I see it's supported by four rods that come out of the tool. But what pushes them?"

"Every press has a booster, a pneumatic cylinder under the base plate that gets compressed when the press closes. When the press reopens, the cylinder pushes the rods and the ring up. Come to the workshop, and I'll show you!"

Amando led Emil to the factory floor, stopping in front of a blanking and forming press at the first stage. A roll of sheet metal fed through guide rollers in sync with the press's rhythm. A forklift with two close-set forks was just removing a die from the press's platform. Four steel rods fell out from the bottom of the die. Amando pointed out the components Emil had questions about.

"See, these are the rods, and there, beneath the die, is the booster cylinder I was talking about," Amando explained, pointing at the machinery with a practiced hand. "When the press goes down, it compresses the air in this cylinder, and as it rises, that pressure forces the rods to push up, ejecting the part from the die."

Emil nodded, feeling a sense of relief and understanding

wash over him, seeing that the die removed from the press looked almost identical to the one Marian gave him to detail.

Emil felt grateful for Amando's support. The willingness of his new colleagues to help made the daunting task ahead seem a little less intimidating. As they walked back to the office, Emil noticed that at the spinning machine, Vini disassembled the rollers from a lateral arm as Mr. Mevison, disappointed followed him toward the lathes area. On his way, Emil saw many dies opened on benches for maintenance and small repairs. Vasile, the king of lathe operators, was still working on his machine and responded to Emil's salute, raising his right hand. It was late and Emil felt little tiredness signs coming to him.

"Thanks, Amando. I appreciate that," said Emil, extending his hand for a shake, and entered the office to take his coat. Going toward his car, thought about the great news to share with Coca. Tonight, they would celebrate. Not just for the six dollars an hour but for the start of a new life, full of promise and hope, a life where their hard work and resilience might finally be rewarded.

"Thanks, God, for such a good day!" he thought again, this time with a deep sense of gratitude.

The Thorn

As Emil unlocked the front door of his apartment, he immediately knew they had guests. Coca came to greet him in the hallway, and as he was hanging his coat on a hanger, she informed him that Traian and his wife were there. Traian and Mioara were their neighbors from the fifth floor, people they had met when they moved into this building. Emil would have preferred not to have visitors at this hour, but given the situation, what could he do? He entered the living room, and Traian, standing in the dining area, greeted him with a beer in hand:

"Hey, Emil, I've been waiting for you here for ages..."

"Hello, Traian. Good evening, Mioara. What's new?"

"Well, what do you think? We heard you started a new job today," Traian said. "How did it go?"

"Not bad. It's a new factory, lots of machines, lots of products. I think it will be alright."

He sat at the table. Coca placed utensils and a glass in front of him. Several empty beer bottles were scattered in the center of the table. Traian filled Emil's glass and gestured to Coca to bring more beer, but Mioara tried to stop him:

"No, Traian, it's late. Emil is tired after a long day. Let's go home now..."

"Let it be, dear; I'm curious to hear how it went. Tell me, how are the bosses? Are they good people?"

"I think so. The one I work with, Marian, gave me some good

instructions. The foreman in the factory, Amando, an Italian, is nice and seems like a decent guy. And the director even raised my salary by another 25 cents on the spot," Emil said, watching their reactions.

Coca, coming in from the kitchen with a pot of hot soup for Emil, asked with surprise:

"But how do you know? This morning, you didn't know how much they would pay you..."

"Shandy, the accountant, told me. The deputy director, Mr. Mevison, had written $5.75 on the employment sheet, but the general director told her to give me six."

"Six dollars?" Traian nearly jumped out of his chair. "Now, with unemployment at 8%? I've been working at my company for over a year and a half, and they've barely given me $4.75. Ah, but that's a reason to celebrate! Bravo, Emil, bravo! To bigger and better things!" Traian exclaimed, downing his glass.

"But what about me, burning my fingers polishing those miserable gold trinkets for three dollars?" Mioara interjected. "Do you know how hard it is to hold those tiny medallions that heat up like hell when you're polishing them? And there's nothing you can do with a supervisor watching you all the time, not letting you take a break... I have a friend who works in an eyeglasses factory, and she gets three dollars, too. If I had more money, I would enroll in a university to reclaim my diploma; it's easier than passing the language test."

"You're right," said Coca. "I'm in the same situation. I've taken the English Proficiency exam twice already and failed. It's really tough."

Saying this, she returned to the oven to take out the next dish for Emil.

"Did you put the kids to bed?" Emil asked her.

"They're in the bathroom, brushing their teeth."

"I didn't see them at all today. I want to spend some time with them. I'll eat and then go check on them."

Mioara and Coca continued discussing the TOEFL English language exam, without which they couldn't have their diplomas recognized by professional organizations. Mioara had started working at a jewelry factory, while Coca worked in a hospital in the surgical tool sterilization department. Both felt frustrated with their situations, though compared to others who couldn't find work at all, they were in a better position. The country was mired in rising inflation and high unemployment.

After Emil went to see what the kids were doing, Traian, left alone, kept drinking beer, bored and frustrated that he had no one to talk to. Eventually, he got up from his chair:

"Do you have another bathroom in this apartment?"

"Yes, in our bedroom. Let me show you!" Coca replied.

They walked through the hallway where the main bathroom and the kids' room were located. At the end of the hallway was the entrance to their bedroom. Coca let Traian in, pointing to which of the two side doors was the second bathroom. Seeing the bed with its cover by the far wall, Traian turned toward Coca and, with a brazen smirk, insinuated:

"So, this is the place where you two...," he trailed off while rudely mimicking a lewd gesture with his hands.

Shocked, Coca instinctively slapped him lightly across the face, her expression revealing both disgust and anger, but she said nothing. A moment later, stunned by her reaction, Traian slapped her back harder, leaving the mark of his hand on her face. Tears welled up in Coca's eyes, and humiliated, unable to speak, she fled into the kitchen.

From the slightly open bathroom door where Emil was with the kids, he heard the commotion in the next room. He sprang out in front of Traian, grabbed him by the collar, and dragged him out. Traian, drunk, grinned foolishly as if nothing had happened, trying to make excuses:

"Come on, man, it was just a joke. Honestly, it was just a joke."

Emil hauled him to the front door, opened it, and shoved him out, disgusted by Traian's attempts to grab onto something to avoid being forcibly removed.

"So, this is how you treat your friends? Huh? Do you think your wife is a saint? I've seen plenty like her, pretending to be saints," Traian shouted as Emil slammed the door.

Emil's hands were trembling with rage as he stood by the door, trying to calm down. Traian's words, "Do you think your wife is a saint?" echoed sharply in his mind like a trumpet in a battle charge. How could he know if Coca was a saint or not? What did that vile man know that he did not?

As Traian continued to shout from the hallway, Mioara appeared in tears, carrying Traian's forgotten coat. She stepped out to calm her husband, pleading with him to stop yelling. A slap rang out loudly from the hallway, followed by more curses. Mioara covered her eyes with her hand, bent over, and began walking slowly toward the elevator, followed by Traian.

Emil didn't want to look at Coca anymore and went straight to their bedroom without saying a word. With mechanical movements, he took his pajamas from under the pillow, where they always were, and went into the bathroom to change. He brushed his teeth, turned off the lights, and lay down in bed. He closed his eyes, but sleep would not come. He remembered how, on the way home, he could hardly wait to tell Coca about his unexpected raise, and now everything seemed shattered. The joy had turned into a heavy sorrow, a sorrow that clung to him like a curse he couldn't shake off. What did that scoundrel Traian mean about Coca? What did that disgusting man know that he didn't? What kind of wife was Coca? Saintly or not, could he at least trust her to be faithful?

When he met her, she was an innocent girl. He knew that because, until that mountain trip they took together, no one else had crossed the Rubicon of her maidenhood. But then, in thirteen years of marriage, who knows what had happened? With small children at home, as she worked mainly afternoon and night shifts in the hospital, how could he really know what she was doing? At first, there was love, a love so intense that no place or distance could interrupt the fluid connection between them, like conjoined twins who share the same sensations even when separated. But that was in the beginning. Then came the children, their needs, the problems, and now he found himself at this point: "Do you think your wife is a saint?"

He felt Coca coming in quietly, pulling her pajamas from under the pillow in the dark and slipping into the bathroom. She came back and lay down next to him, trying not to wake him. He lay turned away from her, motionless, as if trying to spy on her every move. The thorn of doubt tormented him. Everything had been so beautiful until just a moment ago, and now, suddenly, all he could see was darkness. His trust, his certainty, and all his plans for the future seemed to have evaporated with the sound of those words: "Do you think your wife is a saint?"

Emil turned over on his back, staring blankly at the dark ceiling. Beside him, Coca breathed softly in her sleep. On other nights, he might have reached out to gently caress her shoulder or perhaps kiss it, moved by the love he felt for her, love as one holds for an icon. But now... Now?

"What about the children?" he asked himself, shaken by the appearance of this new thought. "They are innocent; they are our children. What should I do if I can't find the answer to this doubt, if the blade of uncertainty keeps cutting deeper into my heart, if the temple I built around her crumbles? Crumbles? Should I let it crumble without any evidence? Then what should I do? Dear God, why am I blinded by this poison that was sown in me through the words of a scoundrel? Have mercy, Lord, help me with some light to guide my steps and show me the way! Help me, Lord, not to destroy what I tried to build. Have mercy on us, Lord, and on our children! Amen!"

The Other Side of the World

When Emil came out of the bathroom in the morning, he found Coca in the kitchen preparing breakfast and sandwiches for the kids and himself. Without saying good morning, he went straight to the cupboard to grab coffee mugs for both. He filled his own and sat down at the table. Coca slid a portion of the omelet, fried on the electric stove, onto a plate and placed it in front of him. He ate in silence while skimming the headlines on the front page of the Toronto Star, to which he subscribed. Then he packed the newspaper and his sandwich into his briefcase, preparing to leave. When he reached the door, Coca came after him to kiss him goodbye:

"What's going on with you today? Is there a problem?"

He let her kiss his cheek but left without saying a word. In his mind, Coca's kiss felt cold, like Judas'. In the elevator, he read all the ads on the walls, trying to shake the thoughts that were tormenting him. He wanted to arrive at work with a clear head, but he wasn't sure he could. He wished he could forget, but he didn't know how. The poison was working…

At the office, he sat in front of the drafting board, attempting to concentrate. He had finished drawing the first detail of Marian's die, and now he needed to write the dimensions next to the measuring lines. On the long table next to him, the 10:1 drawing showed the inner and outer diameters of the product at each stage. Without anyone telling him, Emil deduced from the General Motor reference drawing that the outer diameter, which had tolerances, was more important. But he didn't know if the inner diameter of the part had to match the 10:1 scale or not.

When Marian saw that Emil was absorbed in figuring out how the die worked, he left him alone to find the answers he was searching for. Used to working with soft background music, Marian watched as Emil fidgeted with his pencil, chewing the end, and turned off the radio to avoid disturbing him. He knew Emil would eventually come to ask for help. The only problem was time: they had just 12 weeks from the moment the order came in to produce the prototype. During that time, Marian had to determine the technological process, make the designs for each die and tool, and get them into production. Since he couldn't do all that alone, he needed to hire someone. Emil seemed like the right person so far, but it would have been easier if they had hired someone experienced in tool design. Marian had told Mr. Mevison this, but he had insisted on bringing Emil. Now, Marian wondered what he could do to make Emil a real help. But he wasn't a teacher, and Emil seemed too proud to ask questions. Shortly, he saw Emil approaching him shyly:

"Sorry, Marian. How do I know what size to give the pieces that make up the punch? I see the dimensions at 10:1 and understand the outer diameter is more important than the inner one, but I'm not sure if the punch has the same size as shown in the 10:1 drawing?"

"No! The punch is generally smaller. To better understand this, I think you should read this booklet, which I recommend you buy when you get the chance. All toolmakers say it's their Bible. I call it the toolmaker's primer. Look through it; you'll find answers to most of your questions."

Emil took the pocket-sized silver-covered book and examined it. It was full of sketches and formula. Having just over a hundred pages, included methods for calculating the transition stages of a workpiece during reduction, along with their method of calculation. Not wanting to waste time, Emil took it to the Xerox machine in the administration corridor and copied the cover and a few pages he needed immediately. Patricia, the girl he'd met yesterday, saw him from her desk and waved hello. Emil smiled back. As he entered the office, the bell rang, signaling the first coffee break. He sat down at his desk to delve deeper into the little book. Passing by with a mug in hand, Marian asked:

"Aren't you coming for coffee? You seem down today…"

"Yeah… I don't know what's wrong with me. I don't think I slept well last night."

"Don't worry about your position here if that's what's bothering you. Rest assured, you can't know everything from day one."

"I get it. I'm trying," Emil replied, forcing a bitter smile.

In the cafeteria, a crowd of employees, mostly machine operators, had gathered around the tables. Amidst the hum of foreign words, Emil deduced that most of these employees were Latin

American immigrants. Marian and Emil joined the line at the coffee machine, and a tall, dark-skinned girl sidled up to Marian. She held postcard-sized photos from the company's Christmas party. Marian put an arm around her waist. The girl wrapped her arm around his shoulder, smiling seductively:

"When are you going to dance with me again?"

"I don't know. When I have time."

"Don't you love me anymore?"

"Of course, Sonia. But what will John say?"

"Who cares? He's not my man…"

"What if he hits me? He has a lot of friends here."

"Why didn't you ask that when you went with me after the party?"

"Because you didn't tell me he was your guy," Marian replied, irritated, walking away without the coffee he'd come for.

Sonia stood bewildered for a moment before sitting at a table with other girls.

Left alone, Emil filled two cups of coffee, one black and one with sugar and milk, for Marian and headed back to the office. On the way, he met Amando at his corridor desk.

"Hello, Amando," Emil greeted him.

"Oh, hi! Glad I saw you. I need a 10:1 for the poly-groove. I want to check on the shadowgraph of the rollers Vini ordered. What do you say, Emil? Can you handle that?"

"Yes, but I don't know what you're talking about."

"Haven't seen a shadowgraph yet?"

"No."

"OK. Have your coffee and then come to me. I'll show you!"

Bringing the coffee back, Marian tried to explain himself to Emil:

"That girl, I don't know what she wants from me. I danced with her one night, and now she won't leave me alone. All these Spanish guys are like family. They have brought each other here. It's not good to get mixed up with them..."

Emil told Marian what Amando had asked him to do. After the break, they went together to the quality control department, where several technicians were measuring various pulleys on devices equipped with analytical control tools. Marian stopped in front of a machine with a circular, backlit screen. On the screen was a drawing on tracing paper, showing a 10:1 enlarged V-shape of a pulley for V-belts. Clamped in a vise on the machine's table was a narrow section of a pulley illuminated by a beam of light. By moving the machine's table up, down, or sideways, the pulley's shadow was projected onto the drawing on the screen. If the shadow fit perfectly over the drawing's outline, the part was good.

"See?" Marian said. "Amando wants a similar drawing for the multi-grooves rollers. Remember when Vini used a metal template to check the pulley's grooves? It's easier to see on the shadow graph if the part is good or not. Since the drawing is magnified ten times, the error is reduced ten times. Got it?"

"Yes."

In the office, Marian gave Emil a Ford Motor drawing for a pulley with six channels and short teeth, detailed in a separate ellarged view. After studying the drawing and its dimensions for a few minutes, Emil taped a sheet of tracing paper to the drafting board and began, with thin lines, to draw the sinusoidal shapes of the teeth at a 10:1 scale. When he finished, he called Marian to check the drawing. Marian verified a few dimensions and told Emil to add both the minimum and maximum radii indicated in the Ford drawing. Emil fixed the graphite marks with a colorless spray and took the drawing to the shadow graph. Amando brought a mirror polished roller for poly-grooves pulleys. After installing it on a mount in front of the machine's light beam and focusing its shadow on the screen, they could see the irregularities in it:

"Are you sure you didn't mess up the tooth angles in the drawing?" Amando asked Emil.

"He didn't mess up. I checked," Marian said from behind, having just arrived to see how the roller was made.

"In that case, it's no wonder we can't produce a decent pulley… Email, please call Vinicio here. Tell him to bring the template he used," Amando requested.

Vinicio, interrupted from his work at the same machine where Emil had found him the day before, cursed loudly, complaining that no one let him finish his job. After Amando clamped the template in the vise, it became clear that it was far off from the contour of Emil's drawing. There was no doubt that, up until Amando's intervention, no one had thought to use the shadowgraph. Emil was impressed by the ingenuity of the machine, which, using shadows, revealed flaws invisible to the naked eye through magnification. "Who pays attention to a shadow?" he thought. "Shadows follow us everywhere, but no one values their benefit: all it takes is a lamp and a screen. Move the lamp back and forth, and the shadow grows or shrinks. If you place the face of an angel on the screen, how many beings will have shadows identical to that face? But Coca? Oh no! Coca, with her angelic face, would certainly blend seamlessly with the image on the screen. That's for sure, but is that enough? No! Not a shadow, but something more is needed; a light capable of penetrating the hidden depths of the soul, like an X-ray…"

"Emil, did you understand what Amando wants?" Marian asked.

"No, sorry. I was thinking about something else."

"This 10:1 needs to be multiplied into several copies. We must give it to all our roller suppliers. Otherwise, we can't make proper parts," Amando repeated.

"But do any of them even have a machine like this to be able to use 10:1?" Marian raised the issue.

"If they want to keep getting work from us, they'll have to buy one. We can't do anything with unsuitable rollers," Amando retorted.

Emil pulled Marian aside.

"Tracing paper is not a good medium for 10:1. Its dimensions change with the surrounding temperature and humidity. I suggest we do the drawing on Milar, which is a much more stable and transparent medium. What do you think?"

"Let's see what these guys decide first..."

Emil returned to his desk. He picked up the little silver-covered notebook to reproduce a few more pages on the photocopier to study in his spare time. He asked Megan, the receptionist, where he could find some colored pencils to highlight the text. She got up from her desk, opened the door to a narrow room with shelves on one side, and asked him what colors he wanted. Emil approached the woman, who was bent over a shelf at knee level, and in the dimness of this secluded space, as he tried to distinguish the colors in the boxes, his hand brushed involuntarily her hip. Megan turned, staring silently into his eyes. Then, standing upright before him like a candle awaiting the breath to extinguish its flame, she remained motionless, studying his every feature. Emil felt her breath on his cheeks and stepped back, pointing to the yellow highliner.

In his mind, Coca appeared. Would she have reacted the same way in a similar situation? Megan probably wouldn't have objected if she had been held close or even kissed. And if he had suggested a rendezvous, she might have accepted. But Coca?

After the shift ended, just minutes after Marian had left at three o'clock, feeling unable to focus, Emil walked into the plant, thinking that maybe by observing up close what each machine produced, he could clear his mind. On each die, the flat sheet of metal, like a piece of paper, changed its shape, initially taking the form of a yogurt bowl, only to be transformed in subsequent steps into various shapes with qualities and purposes determined by extreme external forces of the press. As he reviewed these machines, including the spinning machines, Emil reflected that, much like the steel sheets, a person too can be reshaped into something they may never have intended to become when faced with the extreme forces of life. Just like the steel, beaten by the hammer, pressed by machines, or rolled, people too are changed, forced by circumstances beyond their control. With these thoughts running in his head, Emil also left the factory.

In the car, he started the engine and lit a cigarette. He sat in the parking lot until he took the last drag, reluctant to go home. Not wanting to embarrass himself in front of the employees still coming out of the factory, he pulled onto the street and headed toward Highway 7, driving slowly. On the left, he saw a restaurant sign on a house with a large parking area and pulled in. A solid-looking man stood guard outside the massive wooden door.

Inside was a large room with many scattered tables in semi-darkness, a huge bar against the wall near the door, and, at the far end, a brightly lit stage. A few young women, dressed only from the waist down, were serving customers, a mix of men of all ages, chatting and joking with the waitresses, enjoying the view of their variously shaped bare breasts. Emil found an empty table on the edge, near the wall, and ordered a beer.

What he was seeing was unfamiliar: an orgy of naked or barely clothed bodies, some in swimsuits or lingerie, dancing on tables or on the laps of men. Waitresses, half undressed, served tables while on stage, a dozen young girls with immature bodies dressed in white T-shirts and panties lined up under bright lights. The scene looked surreal as if cut from an illustrated book depicting the bacchanals of ancient times. A self-assured man on stage, playing the role of master of ceremonies, asked lewd questions to the girl at the front of the line. With a syringe-shaped pump, he sprayed water on the girl's white shirt, turning it transparent so that her breasts became clearly visible, drawing applause from the audience. The girl—an aspiring actress, perhaps—removed her wet shirt at the man's urging, followed by the rest of her clothes. The other girls followed suit, one by one, all of them young, trusting the deceptive flattery and promises of success, innocent victims of human traffickers.

Emil shuddered, seeing these girls who would end up living a life of slavery in brothels. Sickened and outraged, Emil stood up to leave. As he made his way out, one of the animators stepped in front of him, asking if he wanted a lap dance.

"It's not expensive. Five minutes for ten dollars. If you want a personal service, I have a private room in the back, but that costs twenty."

Emil looked at the girl—a brunette with a chest still bronzed from the summer sun—who didn't seem to be older than twenty. He smiled politely, saying he was in a hurry and left. In his car, he let the engine warm up and turned the radio on loud. He didn't want to think about anything anymore. What he had seen tonight surpassed any imagination, and he felt like he had committed a terrible sin by entering that place where the Devil lured his victims. He would never set foot in that place again. That, he knew for sure.

The Confession

By the time Emil arrived home, it was already dark outside. The children were in the living room, watching a TV program. As he took off his coat in the hallway, Lia, his daughter, came to complain that Ducu, her brother, wouldn't let her watch "Sesame Street". It was the show beloved by all the kids in her class, but Ducu, or Sănducu as she called him, had started watching a western movie, fully absorbed by the action on the screen. From the kitchen, Coca called out, telling him to wash his hands as she had already warmed up dinner. Soothing Lia with a pat on the head, Emil told her to wait until Ducu's film finishes, and then he went into the bathroom.

As he washed, he caught a glimpse of himself in the mirror, as though staring at a stranger, and began talking to his reflection:

"Now what, old man? You tried to avoid it today, and now you don't know what to do… Of all the women in the world, she was your wellspring of purity, the beam of light through which you filtered everything around you, like the halo the sun casts on the dreary houses of a deserted street. Every word from her mouth weighed as much as the truth itself. But now? What's become of it? Was it all a lie? If we go by what that scoundrel Traian from the fifth floor said, she's no saint. So, what is she? What's the difference between her and Megan? Or that girl who offered herself to me for twenty dollars?"

He felt a lump forming in his throat and stepped out of the bathroom. On the kitchen table, his dinner sat waiting on a plate. He started eating, staring at the tablecloth.

"Had a bad day today? Did something go wrong?" Coca asked.

"No. Did the kids finish their homework for tomorrow?" he replied.

"Yes. But why aren't you answering me? Why are you upset?"

"We'll talk later. I want to spend some time with the kids for now."

After he finished eating, he sat on the couch next to Ducu. Lia, like a little kitten craving attention, snuggled under his arm. The Western was still playing on the TV, and Ducu eagerly explained to his father which character was the villain and who the hero was. After finishing the dishes and tidying up the kitchen, Coca told the children it was late, and they needed to get ready for bed. Despite protests and pleas, one by one, the children washed up and went to their room. Finally, alone, Coca sat on the edge of the couch, looking at Emil's profile, his eyes still glued to the screen.

"So, what do you want to talk about?" Coca asked.

"Nothing."

"But you said we'd talk later…"

"I did. But I don't understand why you slapped Traian. What got into you to do that?"

"You weren't there to see what that pig showed me. I never imagined someone could be so disgusting. That's why…"

"What did he show you?"

Coca mimicked Traian's obscene gesture from the previous evening.

"That's not enough," Emil said after understanding the gesture's meaning. "Traian felt bold enough to pull that stunt because there's been some sort of familiarity between you two before. And you slapped him for the same reason. What happened before last night?"

Coca's eyes filled with tears.

"Nothing, Emil, absolutely nothing! Don't think the worst of me! Yes, he tried, I won't lie, but nothing happened."

"What did he try?"

"He tried to… have me. Last week, I called Mioara because

I needed some parsley for the soup, and I didn't have any. Traian answered.

'Is Mioara home?' I asked.

'Yes. But what's wrong?' he asked.

'Oh, nothing. I just need some parsley. Can I come to get some?'

'Sure, no problem,' he said. I got off the elevator on the fifth floor, and Traian was waiting with the apartment door open. I stepped in, and he closed the door behind me.

'Where's Mioara?'

'She'll be right back,' he replied.

'I don't have time, the food on the stove. Just give me some parsley.'

'I'll give it to you, but sit down for a minute. I need to tell you something…'

'What do you want to say? I don't have time now; the kids will be home soon.'

'Oh, come on, sit for a second, it won't take long.'

'Tell me what you want to say; I'm listening.'

'You really don't want to sit down?'

'No!' I saw him try to grab my hand to pull me onto the couch, so I backed up to the wall, reaching for the door handle. He leaned over me, pressing both hands against the wall.

'If you don't give me a kiss, I won't let you go,' he said.

'Traian, stop joking. Are you giving me the parsley or not?'

'Only if you let me kiss you.'

He kept me pinned against the wall by the door. I was trapped between his arms. I tried to push him away to free myself from his grip, but he threw his weight on me. He held my head with one hand to kiss me while using the other to block my left arm. I don't know how he managed to grab my arm behind my back, and with his other hand, he started groping my chest. Pinned against the wall, immobilized by his weight, he searched for my mouth while lifting my skirt with his free hand, trying to slip it inside my panties. I was desperate, and I didn't know what to do, alone there with an animal like him.

'Stop! Calm down! You're an animal; God will punish you!'

'What? You're pretending to be a saint now? Since when are you a saint?'

When I saw, he was trying to drag me to the couch, I managed to grab the door handle, open it, and scream as loud as I could for help. That saved me. I could hear voices near the elevator, and I kept screaming, 'Help! Help!'

Then he let me go with that disgusting smirk of his, saying, 'What, darling? Go on, I'm not holding you…'"

"That's all that happened," Coca concluded her story.

"And why was he here last night?" Emil asked.

"Mioara called earlier to ask if she could come over, so they both came. I never imagined I'd have to face him again, but when I saw him, I didn't know what to do. I felt bad for Mioara, so I kept quiet."

The news played on the TV, unnoticed. Emil sat rigidly, fists clenched on his knees, saying nothing. Coca's confession stirred him deeply, and he wanted to go upstairs to the scoundrel on the fifth floor and strangle him. But he knew that wasn't the solution. Then what was?

He remembered a man he knew in his youth who had served twelve years in prison for strangling his wife after catching her in bed with another man. The man had become a broken shell, cast aside by life, because even after his release, he continued to serve a sentence, one of conscience, for the sin he had committed in front of God. Back home in Romania, there was a certain cult among some men. Bragging over drinks, fueled by novels from the time about women glorifying a real man, they would try to seduce more women to fill the importance of the man they considered themselves to be. So, like modern-day Casanovas, each devotee of this theory kept a tally of the women they had conquered. This archaic cult might still exist today, but it has caused many tragedies and torn apart many families.

"Why didn't you tell me about this incident with Traian earlier?"

"I don't know. Fear. I was afraid of what you might do. I just want us to live in peace, not in hatred. What are you going to do?"

"I don't know. Go to bed; I need some time to think," Emil said.

"Emil, I have a bad feeling. Please, listen to me. Don't seek revenge! Forgive that scoundrel who came on to me. I forgave him."

"You forgave him? Maybe you liked what he did to you? That's the real problem… After all that happened, you let him into our house and served him drinks. Why? To give him the chance to repeat the insult, which is exactly what happened? Forgive him? Let him go to hell! But you? I can't forgive you!"

"Oh, Emil, how cruel you are. You know just how to break my heart," Coca said, leaving the room with tears streaming down her face.

Emil remained on the couch, and somehow, without

realizing it, he was still there when dawn broke, shivering from the cold in front of the television, which was still playing.

The Three Lives

In the following days, nothing changed in the Ciubaru household. The cold distance between the parents started to affect their children, who were unaccustomed to seeing them so silent, not speaking directly to each other. Emil had taken to sleeping in the living room, moving his pajamas and toiletries to the bathroom down the hall, and he began returning home late at night. Coca continued to manage the groceries, the children's lessons, and all that was necessary, but the previous cheerfulness was gone. Her eyes were often filled with tears, and the children, witnesses to these scenes, grew quiet and withdrawn, sensing it wasn't the time to cause their parents more distress.

Even the television was used less during the day. Only in the evenings, when Emil returned home, did they gather around it on the couch, sometimes already in their pajamas, buzzing like bees around a flower while muted images flashed across the screen. Coca would finish tidying up in the kitchen and come to hurry them off to bed. Then, she would retire to the bedroom. Left alone, Emil would go to the wardrobe by the entrance to look for the pack of cigarettes he'd left in a pocket and the bed linen to spread over the couch. He hadn't been in the habit of smoking indoors before, but now the need for a cigarette seemed essential. He was angry at himself for not being able to control the simmering rage that had built up inside him in recent days. He waited for a miracle, but it was slow to arrive.

He entered the bathroom to change, and once again, face to face with the mirror, he looked at his unshaven face, red eyes, and hair suddenly graying at the temples. With critical eyes, he analyzed his reflection—he appeared tired, weak, and powerless, like a wreck left adrift at sea.

"Emil, boy, wake up! This life isn't for you! Take the helm and fight the storm if you want to make it through!"

He knew it was easy to say but hard to do. He was living two lives in one, or maybe even three. At the factory, he had completed the poly-groove design onto the Milard at a scale of 10:1 in multiple copies, which would become the standard for the execution of multi-groove pulley rollers and sent to suppliers. After Vinicio tried to fix a defective roller himself on a lathe, Amando had asked Vasile, the king of lathe operators, to see what he could do. Vasile was truly a master; somehow, the roller he reworked matched the contour of the design perfectly. However, it broke during the first test. The steel it was made from was too brittle. The factory's manager, Mr. Mevison, called in representatives from the steel mills that supplied materials, and they devised a recipe for a special steel.

After introducing the shadowgraph as a tool for verifying the poly-groove, a breeze of hope for success swept through the factory's leadership; around the machine where Vinicio was trying to create this pulley, more and more people and engineers from outside were brought in to oversee, discuss, and test different solutions. After the eight-hour workday ended, only a few of those assisting with the project went home. In the evening, around six, trays of food, sandwiches, pizza, or chicken schnitzels with fries and Coca-Cola were brought to the dining hall, and work continued.

Emil was glad he could stay longer at work because he felt uncomfortable with the silence and coldness in his own home. He had finished the details of his first die and was eagerly waiting for Marian to review them. In a way, this would be his trial by fire, not just from a technical drawing perspective but also in terms of how well he understood the way the component parts worked together in the process.

Marian, very methodically, took his blueprint copies and began checking each dimension and tolerance in order. During this time, Emil started studying the next die design, keeping one eye on what Marian was reviewing next to him. He couldn't see the notes Marian was making on the drawings, and, impatient like a student in front of a teacher, he waited for either approval or disapproval of his work. When the clock announced the end of the shift at three o'clock, Marian rolled up the drawings and handed them to Emil:

"Except for a few notes I made on some of places, you did a good job."

While getting ready to leave, Gerry, the general manager, entered the office. Seeing Marian about to leave, he asked:

"Where are you going? We might need you here."

"I can't stay. I have to leave."

"Where are you going? Don't you see the battle being fought here?"

"I see it, but I need money. That's why I'm going to work somewhere else where they pay me better."

"They can't pay you better than we do for overtime."

"I'm not talking about overtime. They're offering me a salary I don't get here—12 dollars an hour."

"Twelve dollars? What are you waiting for? Go, work for them! Goodbye!" Gerry said as he walked out.

Marian, bewildered, took off his coat and returned to his desk. Emil, sitting at his drafting board, watched in shock at how quickly the situation had turned. These events would have repercussions for him, too. It was hard to predict what would happen in the coming days.

"You can't leave like this," he told Marian. "When people

are angry, they say things they later regret. Come to work tomorrow like nothing happened!"

"Be serious. Tomorrow, they'll chase after me, begging me to come back. You'll see. In any case, if they give you something to do, you should tell them you don't know how to make it. You're new here. Got it?"

Emil silently watched as Marian gathered his things, stuffing them into plastic bags. He glanced around the office one last time, put his coat and hat back on, and shook Emil's hand before leaving.

"Just tell them this: 'I don't know how to do this!' Got it?" And he left.

Alone in the office, Emil felt the weight of an enormous burden pressing down on him, crushed by its pressure, combined with the tension of the situation at home, as if under the ominous alignment of fate's dark stars. The rumor of Marian's departure from the factory spread quickly, and Amando was the first to come and inquire. Emil offered brief explanations, still shocked by the swift exchange of words with the general director and Gerry's resolute refusal to be manipulated by Marian.

"What do you plan to do?" Amando asked him.

"I don't know. I'll do what I can and the rest, whatever God wills."

"You'll manage. I'm sure! We'll be here for you whenever you need help. Don't worry..."

"Thanks, Amando."

Emil rested his head on his arms at his desk, pondering how easily people offer assurances they don't even believe in themselves. He didn't notice that Shandy had entered, coat and purse in hand, asking what had happened. She placed her things on Marian's desk and sat on Emil's; one foot propped on the edge of his chair. As if waking from another world, he raised his head and looked at the girl beside him.

"You came to pity me?"

"Not at all. I came to lift your spirits."

"My spirits? What can you do to lift my spirits?"

"Who knows? Maybe something important, or maybe nothing at all. Ask, and it shall be given to you, as the Bible says."

Emil continued to look into Shandy's eyes. They were as clear as the sky on a splendid summer day. Next to him on the chair, her foot, emerging from a rubber slipper, seemed to tempt his hand, starved lately by Coca's coldness. He stroked her ankle at first, then her calf. When he reached her knee, he encountered the hem of her black wool skirt and slipped his hand underneath, touching her warm, soft skin. Shandy didn't react at all, continuing to meet his gaze as if they were both spellbound by the same captivating enchantment. Emil, rising from his chair, took Shandy by the hand and led her to the darker area behind the drafting boards near the window and back office wall. Here, they could kiss without fear of being seen by anyone. Her entire body responded obediently to his advances, and no vocabulary in the world could adequately express their passion for this unexpected love affair.

Three lives in one. He continued to stare at his reflection in the children's bathroom mirror, and, for the first time, it seemed to him that the face staring back wasn't his own but Traian's. He began to realize that, in fact, there was no difference between him and Traian. Unbelievably, after thirteen years of marital fidelity, he, Emil Ciubaru, was no longer the loyal and honest man he once was but a despicable scoundrel, no better than Traian.

"Bravo, boy! Congratulations! You've joined the fine company!"

Nirvana

"Good morning, Shandy!"

"Hi, Emil!" Shandy replied, waving at someone from the car she had just stepped out of in the factory parking lot.

Emil kept walking along the sidewalk toward the factory entrance. Shandy caught up to him:

"Emil, can you give me a ride home tonight? My husband needs the car; he's going to Ottawa today."

"I don't know what I'm doing yet. Now that I'm alone, I'm afraid they'll bring someone else in my place."

"I don't think they'll get rid of you, but they might hire someone else. Anyway, we'll talk later," Shandy said as Emil held the door open for her.

In the office, Emil unrolled the blueprints Marian had reviewed the day before. Mostly, there were a few notes about dimensioning styles and the size of some tolerances. Emil was relieved that there weren't any errors needing correction before they could go into production. Amando stopped by briefly to say good morning, and then Vasile appeared:

"Is it true what I heard last night? Marian was fired?"

"I'm afraid so. I told him to come in today as if nothing had happened, but he said they would send someone to bring him in," Emil replied.

"No chance. With their money, they can hire anyone. They won't send for him. But what happened?"

Emil told Vasile how the conversation with Gerry had unfolded in the office. Vasile paused for a moment, thinking:

"It won't be easy for him. He had some personal projects but nothing major. He boasted that others offered him twelve dollars an hour. With overtime here, he could've made a lot of money, but he got caught up in those projects…"

Mr. Mevison appeared during their conversation, and Vasile, excusing himself, headed back to his lathe. The manager couldn't help but make a slightly ironic remark:

"Is the Romanian gang having a problem?"

After a moment of hesitation, Emil replied:

"No. But Marian's firing shocked many."

"So, do we need to hire someone else, or can you manage on your own?"

"I don't know yet. I haven't had time to assess the workload. Give me a few days to get an idea, then I'll let you know."

"OK! If you need anything, come to me. Anytime."

Alone again, Emil sat down at his drafting board. During the time he had spent with Marian, he had learned many new things about dies, the special steels used, the hardness of materials for forming or cutting, and a wealth of information about the workshops that made the tools. He realized that time was of the essence and knew he had to find a quick solution to finish the details as fast as possible. But what solution? And how could he be sure his dimensions and tolerances would work?

In the corner of the office, near the wall, stood two or three cardboard boxes filled with old original drawings for dies and other tools in production. Each compartment was labeled with the order number of each product made. Emil realized that the answers to his future problems lay in those boxes. By studying how certain issues had been resolved in those drawings, he could find solutions to the challenges that would inevitably arise to him.

With this in mind, he spread out on the table the assembly drawing of the next tool, which needed to be detailed, part by part, into smaller individual drawings. The die consisted of almost thirty components, each requiring views and sections that would explain how every part contributed to the overall function. Some of them were simple, concentric parts that could stand one on top of other like a tower. Those could be detailed together on the same drawing in assembly, easy-to-read and execute. Emil decided to pursue this approach.

He unrolled the tracing paper on his board and began working. He decided to leave for later what kind of base plates to be ordered and start grouping the pieces that could be drawn together. Choosing to start with the outer bottom rings for first subassembly for execution, he saw that this method sped up his progress.

At lunchtime, Amando came by to check on Emil's mood. Emil made room for him to stand in front of the drafting board.

Amando was the first to see what Emil had accomplished:

"What do you think? Will it work?" Emil asked.

Amando didn't answer immediately.

"You have four pieces here, one on top the other. How will you distribute this to four different people?"

"Each person gets a copy of this drawing and makes their assigned piece. When they're assembled, they have to fit together."

"If you think it can be done this way, go ahead, and we'll see what comes of it," Amando said.

"Amando, you understand I don't have time to do it any other way?"

"I understand. I agree with you. Keep going!"

Relieved, Emil went to the cafeteria to grab a cup of coffee. As the machine poured hot coffee into his cup, Sonia, the worker Marian had argued with a few days earlier, approached him:

"Hey, where's your friend?"

"Which friend? I don't really have friends here."

"The one who brought you into the company, Marian."

"He didn't bring me. I came on my own."

"Doesn't matter. Where is he?"

"I don't know. He doesn't work here anymore."

"Do you have his phone number or address?"

"No, I'm sorry. But what happened?"

"A baby happened. But don't tell anyone."

"No, how do you know it's his?" Emil thought he saw a tear in Sonia's eye.

"I know... because there was no one else before him or after him," she said.

"Then why did you do it?"

"I don't know... I believed him. I wanted a better life..."

Emil looked at her with genuine sympathy.

"That's what the girls back home say too... They do anything for a better life and end up with a worse one. As I said, I'm really sorry, but I don't know anything about him."

"If you find out, will you tell me?"

"Generally, I don't like to get involved in these kinds of things". But after a moment of hesitation, he added, "If I hear something, I'll let you know."

Sonia silently mouthed a thank you. Emil could see the sincerity in her eyes.

Back in the office, Emil resumed his intense work at the drafting board. When he reached the point of dimensioning some pieces with rounded angles, he used measurements at the intersection points of the surfaces, something Marian had never employed. These intersecting angles were crucial for the trapezoidal shape of the drive belts with a 36-40-degree opening.

Toward the end of the day, Shandy came to ask him:

"You're still here? I thought they'd sent you home."

"Don't joke. The day isn't over yet..."

"Alright. Are you giving me a ride home, then?"

"Don't you have work for another hour or two?"

"I think I do. I can stay another hour or two. How are you holding up? Do you think you can manage alone?"

"I don't know yet. Do you know where I can find a wall calendar with all the days of the month so I can plan the important dates?"

"Yes, that's called a planner. I can order one for you. Do you want it for onc month or two?"

"Two would be better."

After the shift change, when the evening crew began work, Mr. Mevison stopped by Emil's office.

"Did you send out the die completed yesterday?"

"I sent the drawings to three suppliers. I'm waiting for their price quotes."

"Was the material ordered?"

"Yes. I gave Norm a note this morning."

"Good job! And now, what are you working on?"

"The redraw die. To save time, I started detailing in assembly, as you can see here..." Emil stepped aside to make room for the boss to look at what he had done. Mr. Mevison, with the same unreadable face, stood silently in front of the drafting table for a while.

"If you don't make any mistakes, this system could work. It will take some time for the workers to get used to it. Some would bring objection."

After the director left, Emil went to pick up Shandy. In the car, she directed him where to go. Her house wasn't exactly in the same direction as his; it was in a neighborhood on the opposite edge of the city. When they arrived, she invited Emil inside. He hesitated to enter her home:

"I don't think it's a good idea. Someone might see us, and I don't want to cause problems for you at home."

"Don't be silly. My husband and I live freely."

"What do you mean, freely?"

"It's a long story. Come in, and I'll tell you."

They entered. Emil was somewhat disappointed by the first impression. It wasn't what he considered a comfortable home despite the many valuable items scattered around. The mess, clothes left everywhere, cigarette butts in plates and ashtrays, and even leftover food from the previous day gave him a bad feeling. Shandy tried to tidy up the small table in the living room before bringing out glasses, a bottle of whiskey, and a plate of chips with a whitish sauce as a snack to go with the drinks. She sat next to him on the couch, took off her shoes, and stretched her legs over Emil's knees.

"If you want to hear our story, fill those glasses with whiskey."

Emil poured the alcohol into both glasses and handed her a glass. He then leaned against the back of the couch, looking at the woman in front of him, stretched out on the couch, her head resting on a hand propped on the back. The temptation to touch her legs seemed natural to him, like an invitation to dance, and the volatile aroma in the glass gently swirled his senses, igniting in him the desire to hold her in his arms. He placed the glass on the table in front of him, then slipping his arms under the woman's body, he picked her up, feeling the direction of the bedroom by intuition. He laid her lightly on the bed, slowly undressed her, one by one, and they made love. She then went naked like a nymph to fetch cigarettes and a bottle of whiskey and sat down in bed next to him again.

"What did you mean you and your man have a free life?" asked Emil.

"Everybody has his own life with us. He can sleep with whoever he wants, and so can I."

"How so? Aren't you jealous when you see him with another woman?"

"Not now. I used to be."

"What happened?"

"He was working at a large company with branches all over the world and he was frustrated that others were always getting promoted and he wasn't. One day, he gets the idea to invite his direct boss to the dinner. We lived then in a modest apartment. I prepared with all the goodies we could afford, and the guy came on the day. We sat down at the table, clinked glasses, and my husband got up, apologizing to the boss for forgetting the secret file open in the office and leaving me alone in the house with that guy. I didn't know what to do. I tried to be nice like a good host, but it wasn't long before the guy moved closer to me, embraced and kissed me against my opposition, and ended defiling me like the last whore in the world. He had me down on the bare floor, then wiped himself with the table napkin and left. I thought of killing myself."

Shandy lay across the nightstand at the end of the bed and poured more whiskey into her glass:

"My husband came into the house moments after his boss left. Apparently he watched from the street corner to see when the guy was gone. His only concern when he came in, was to find out if the boss had been satisfied. He wanted to know what the boss said and if he liked us. In my state, I took the plates from the table and threw them at him. He said I was crazy and left again. I did not count. I hated him for that, God, how I hated him! The boss also came to our place at other times, and my husband always left us alone. He finally got the promotion, but with it, new bosses took his place. From now on, nothing mattered; where the little mouse made its way, the big one could also pass. I started doing the same. Why would I resist the advances of one or the other? I then discovered that there were other open couples like us and even clubs where everyone let their partner sleep with whoever they wanted. That's how I got here."

"Why did you choose to stay with him? Are you satisfied; do you still love him?" Emil asked.

"What was I supposed to do? I no longer had parents and no other siblings. At first, I hated myself for not being able to stand up to that guy. I thought the story of Bob, my husband, forgetting the open cabinet in the office was true. I could not imagine that there was an understanding between them. But when I saw how he reacted, I was disgusted. The abomination of him, of me, of everything. I wanted to leave, but I had nowhere to go. I came to believe that this was my fate. Do you understand? What are we but toys before fate? As for love, I don't know if I love him anymore. But we have to accept ourselves as we are, floating leaves in a stream with not direction. That's life!" Shandy concluded philosophically.

"You know what's curious?" she continued after a while: "I started to agree with Bob. He believes that sex should be free; you sleep with whoever you like. Between the spouses there must be no right of ownership over the other person. It doesn't matter who I've had sex with; when I'm with him, I'm the same as always, with no difference from what I was before. I didn't take anything that was his. Don't you think so?"

Emil remained in thought, following the trail of smoke from the cigarette in his hand. Then he got off the bed to get dressed:

"Where are you going at this hour? Won't you stay with me tonight?"

"I can't. I didn't see my children today. I have to go."

"Too bad. I was going to give you Nirvana, but you don't even know what it's about..."

"Maybe Nirvana is a little different for me than is for you," Emil said before leaving.

In the car, Emil absentmindedly droved the highway that at this hour was not too crowded. Surely, the children would have been put to bed by now, and a strange sense of guilt had settled in. It had been a feeling for a long time, but never as persistent as tonight. He had the impression that everything he touched in his own house, always kept in perfect order and cleanliness, was stained with the germs he brought from outside, from this vicious environment into which he alone entered. It was not enough that he had defiled the purity of his feelings for his children and his wife, whom he had never loved more than at this moment, but what he had seen and learned from Shandy tonight deepened that sense even more. Guilt and shame. No tangent, no degree of comparison could even remotely bring these two beings closer together. Coca and Shandy. The cleanliness, the love, the care with which Coca devoted herself to him and the well-being of the family, sacrificing her own needs for peace, were diametrically opposed to what he could find in Shandy.

The story of this woman, Shandy, disturbed him deeply. None of the poor-quality novels about women depraved and exposed to the worst dehumanizing abuses seemed to him as sinister as the story of Shandy, forced by her own husband to prostitute herself for a better position in the company where he works. It was hard for him to imagine the shock and disappointment she felt when she discovered that the man she trusted and loved could sell her as a commodity to some chiefs for personal use. In her position, Emil thought, it's a wonder she can still function as a normal person. Outside, in spite of the air she breathes, her life resembles a beautifully arranged shop window in a deserted village. She has no one close to her and no impetus on which to rest her hopes. She floats on the surface of a vast lake whose shores cannot be seen at all. She knows she's going to drown, but she keeps flailing her arms and legs. Who wants to live like that?

Driving down the highway with still visible traces of snow, Emil was happy that despite all his inherent troubles, the repeated dismissals since he arrived in the New World, and all the troubles he went through, his existence was full; he received and returned love and that gave him courage every day to start over with more strength, gave him faith that he was on the right path and helped him to always remain an optimist convinced that at the end, everything would turn alright. The fullness of these feelings was due to a single person who became a source of inspiration that transformed him from an insignificant creature into a man, just like in the fairy tale where a frog became a handsome prince. His fairy tale was Coca.

Thinking about her now, he felt a pain drowning him. A heartache combined with shame, as if he had committed a crime to which he never could confess. He wished he could find the strength to go home, lay his head in her lap, and confess everything to her. He wanted to confess, but he knew he couldn't; the risk of losing everything would be too great. He who accused her of dishonesty, how can he go to her, a true saint, to tell her that he has allowed himself to be lured by the fascinations of hell, that he has partaken of its poisoned fruits and now repentant comes to ask her forgiveness? Only in her forgiveness did Emil see the only salvation he needed.

When he entered the apartment, Coca appeared from the living room with eyes that wanted to know if everything was okay, without saying the implied words. There was no rebuke in her look, only the traces of concern for waiting had caused. And the manifestation of love of the past days when he was greeted from the threshold with a kiss, did not take place either. Embarrassed, Emil, without saying a word, headed to the kitchen where the table was waiting for him. While Emil resumed his usual place at the table, Coca put the food on heat. Emil grabbed her hand and pulled the chair next to him for her to sit down:

"Do you have any idea what Nirvana means?"

Coca looked at him, amazed by the question, not knowing what to think:

"Nirvana? Isn't that place in the Buddhist faith where happiness is complete?"

"Exactly! Nirvana is that place. Coca, God has blessed us,

we have known Nirvana. We have been happy every moment since we met, and I don't want to lose this happiness now. Forgive me for the grief I caused you after that incident of the past few days! I was angry, I was hurt by your insult in our house, and I hated to death the meanness of that so-called friend who came to you, but I never once questioned your fairness. Forgive me, dear, for all the suffering because I did not behave properly, and because of me, we all felt the pain of resentment between us."

In Coca's eyes blossomed the crystal balls of tears rolling down her cheeks.

"The days that have passed since then have opened my eyes. My anger, loneliness, and insecurity pushed me to places I could not describe, and I had no idea they existed. Coca, when I saw what was happening in these places, around us and in other homes, I felt sick. I'm not lying! I come back to you sick, with my soul torn by the mess around, and I wonder, with all sincerity, how long we can resist and even our children until the rotting around will also encompass our home. I'm afraid, my dear, I'm afraid, and only you can save us. No one but you can keep us as we still are, unadulterated in our purity. Do you understand, my dear? I want Nirvana back!"

The painting on the easel

We met by chance at the exhibition in front of the city hall in Toronto. This exhibition of paintings by amateurs takes place every year, among other cultural events. I was there with my wife, Valeria, to encourage a lady, the mother of our family doctor, from whom I also bought a painting of hers, a still life. The incident took place years before the pandemic, on a summer Sunday morning. After meeting our doctor's mother and admiring her creations, with one of her paintings under my arm, we continued to visit other booths, and I suddenly saw on a canvas the portrait of a young woman with eyes expressing tender warmth and a special delicacy of features. I stood there admiring the painting on the easel, and from behind me, an elderly man, tall, slightly bent from behind, approached me without saying a word. Leaning against the legs of the nearby tripod were two or three other paintings that he was trying to bring out, although none had caught my eyes like the one I stopped at.

"How much is this painting?" I asked.

"Sorry, this one is not for sale." the man answered me.

"Too bad I would have bought this one."

"Regret. I can't part with this one. She's my daughter."

"I congratulate you. She is beautiful. I can see that this

portrait was made with a lot of love."

"And a lot of pain, dear sir. My daughter passed among the saints a year ago. I could not save her. She developed muscular dystrophy. She could no longer even hold the brush in her hand. She also painted like me. I have her canvases here."

Indeed, the young woman's paintings were completely different in style, showing a more modern conception and exuberant color. That's how I met Grigore Gornescu, an engineer in the field of molecular physics and a professor in Canada, who, due to health problems in his youth, began to paint landscapes from the country of Bihor during his convalescence. Now, after retirement, to pass the time, he started painting again.

He came here from London. Ontario. He heard about this outdoor exhibition, got in his car with his paintings, and came to Toronto. He didn't know how long he would stay in the square here, in front of the town hall, and he asked me if I knew a cheap motel somewhere nearby because across the street, at the Sheraton hotel, the price would be too high. I exchanged a glance with my wife and invited him to sleep at our place. Since our kids were married and in their own homes, we lived alone in a house that was too big for the two of us and had two unused bedrooms. I gave him the address and told him we were waiting for him. He came near the evening hour. My wife was just preparing dinner, but he excused himself by saying that he had eaten. I insisted that he sit with us at the table and bringing a bottle of whiskey and three glasses, the man accepted.

"How was today? Did you sell anything?"

"Just like in our city, people come to see, not to buy. However, I gave two landscapes. There were many who asked about the portrait of my daughter."

"Yes. It is incredibly beautiful. Talking eyes. It's like she wants to say something."

"I think she looked more like your wife," Vali, my wife, chimed in as she arranged the plates on the tablecloth.

"No. Not at all. My wife was beautiful, but Angi, Angela, had only been raised by us. We adopted her when she was little. My father-in-law, a priest, found her on the steps of his house one morning. He didn't know who brought her there. Lena, my wife, had just lost a child. She worked in a lab at the Academy, and none of her colleagues could complete a pregnancy normally. Only later did we realize this. My father-in-law then came to us with this little girl in his arms. Since then, we have not parted with her. Until last May when the Lord took her to Him."

"I'm sorry. I shouldn't have brought up the subject," I said. "Better tell us how you met your wife."

Mr. Gornescu's face lit up with a smile:

"It's a funny story. I was a student at the Polytechnic, but at the same time, I was taking drawing lessons at a Community Art School. It was the grape harvesting season, and I was supposed to meet after classes with my friends Nicu, Emil, and Georgica at the restaurant next to the site of the old circus opposite the University. We found a table in the shade of the garden, sipped the juice from the clay jugs, and devoured the goat pastrami, still sizzling on the plate with fresh polenta. A group of young girls appeared at the next table, one prettier than the other. All our attempts to enter the conversation with them ricocheted bitterly in their royal disregard for us. Georgica, the most well-versed Don Juan of our group, with lessons well learned from his two older sisters, mastered the most effective tricks to conquer women but could not arouse the interest of any of them. Not even a single smile. To my right, at the girls' table, was a blonde with blue eyes and a classic profile. She was slim-waisted, tucked into a blue flowery dress, and was more reserved than the others. I liked her from the first moment. Instinctively, I picked up the drawing pad resting on the leg of my chair, placed it open on my knee, and began to pencil the profile of this girl. One of them noticed what I was doing and started nudging the others. With every moment, I felt the pressure building around me. My friends were making admiring glances at what I was working on, and the girls were getting more curious. At one point, the girl on my right asked,

"Can I see the drawing too?"

I blushed with emotion. More of a shame. I could not concentrate enough, and it seemed impossible to coordinate my hand as if it were not mine. Not a line, not an arch of her fine features, could I faithfully reproduce on the block page. I knew I could not let her see what I had done, and in a panic, I tried a ploy:

"Only if you promise to see me tonight."

The girl scanned me with a piercing gaze,

"Where?"

"Across the street, at the University clock."

"When?"

"At half past six. Is that okay?"

"What's your name? But I want to see the drawing now."

I got up and went to her with an outstretched hand:

"Greg. My name is Grigore Gornescu. I am a student."

"Lena. Where is the drawing?"

"I cannot show it to you now. It's not ready. You will see it tonight. I promise!"

I was crazy. I had no plan, I had no money, and looking at my Russian watch, Pobeda, I realized that I had less than three hours until our meeting. What am I doing? I parted ways with my friends after borrowing some money and ran to catch the tram. At my hostess's home, I showered and changed my clothes. I opened the sketchbook and tried to touch up the shadows on the drawing I started at the restaurant. Slowly, patiently, the image began to appear closer to the memory of her magical face. Finished, I fixed the graphite marks with a spray so that it does not smudge, rolled up the drawing, and wrapped it with a white sheet of paper. I left home at 5 o'clock. I got off the tram at the bridge in front of the Operetta Theatre. I walked down Calea Victoriei and tried to see if I could find tickets at the Comedy Theater behind the Post Office. The most praised show of the season, "The Celebre 702", played there with famous actor Radu Beligan, was my best choice. I don't know who wrote the piece, but people were curious to see it. It was about a prisoner from Sing-Sing in America, sentenced to death. He continued to live because he began to write down his memories. A publishing house postponed his execution, forcing him to finish the book faster. It had to appear on the day of the execution with a banner that read: "The author electrocuted today!" At the ticket counter, a notice announced that the show was sold out for tonight. Disappointed, I wondered what chance I would have of finding two extra tickets among the audience this evening before the show. I got out into the street, and I saw Radu Beligan, the actor, walking towards the entrance that led to the backstage of the theater. I ran after him, shouting:

"Master, master, please!"

The actor stopped looking at me.

"Master," I said excitedly. "Tonight, I am meeting the most beautiful woman I have ever seen in my life. I need two seats for your show. Please! I'll pay for them in gold!"

The actor gave me an understanding smile, taking out a pen from his coat:

"With gold, you say? Then give me something to write on."

I had Lena's drawing rolled up in my hand. He took my role and wrote on the white paper I wrapped the drawing in:

"Two seats, please, front, at tonight's performance," he signed and dated.

I could not believe it! He patted me on the shoulder and winked, saying,

"Good luck tonight!"

"Thank you, master. You saved me!"

That evening at the theater, the usher brought us two chairs, one behind the other, on passage between rows of seats closer to the stage. As the curtain fell at the end, the Famous 702, the actor Radu Beligan, smiled at us from the stage while the applause never stopped."

While our guest was sharing his story, the three of us ate, but I don't remember what because Mr. Gornescu, with his gift of storytelling, conquered us to such an extent that we could have eaten the spoons without noticing. After coffee and dessert, with empty glasses of wine, I asked him if the girl liked the drawing:

"She looked at it during the break. I think she wanted to tease me with questions like, "Why, do I have such a big nose?" On the way out after the show, it was pouring rain outside. We waited for a while under the entrance canopy, and then I took her hand, and we started to run. I tried to protect the drawing under my coat but realizing that Lena was only wearing a summer dress, I gave her my jacket. By the time we reached the tram, both of us were soaked. We wanted to keep the Master's note on the cover of the drawing, but the ink spread so that we could not distinguish his writing. The drawing did not have a better fate either. I went with Lena to her uncle's house on Șerban Vodă Street, where she lived. When we arrived, it was still raining, and I was cold, but I did not feel it. I was holding her by the waist in front of the gate, looking into her eyes because I wanted to believe that she would come to meet me again the next day. I was in love, and I did not know if she felt the same way. We parted with a single kiss of encouragement".

"Did she come?"

"No! I waited an hour. In those days, there were no telephones like there are now, and only a few people had access to one. I didn't know where she worked, and I didn't know what happened. I suspected she didn't like me. I knew where she lived, and I could have written to her, but I did not, although I could not get her out of my mind. One afternoon, I took a notebook and started sketching. Line by line, the face that kept coming to my mind, Lena's face, began to take shape. It turned out better than the first one. When it was done, I put it between two cardboard sheets in an envelope and put it in the mail. A few days later, the landlady told me that a young lady had been looking for me and left me a note. I read a few words:

"I was sick with a fever. I couldn't leave the house. My work phone is... Call me before 4:00. Lena."

"I couldn't wait for time to pass faster until I spoke to her on the phone. I went to wait for her at the exit. She appeared with the happiest smile I had ever seen. She had to go to the preparatory courses for admission to college. She tried the year before but failed. She knew she didn't stand a chance since her family was outcasted for her bourgeoise past. Then, her uncle spoke to an acquaintance at this laboratory within the Academy. She started there as a laboratory assistant. Quickly, she learned what she had to do, she worked with pleasure, and soon she became an assistant in the research group of a lady who led the work in the laboratory. That led her to become a chemist."

Mr. Gornescu took out a pack of cigarettes from his pocket and asked if we minded if he smoked. Although I hadn't smoked in a long time, with the window open, I told him to go ahead. Looking around, he asked us:

"It's late. Aren't I boring you?"

"Not. On the contrary. Keep going!"

Vali finished cleaning and sat down at the table.

"I think there's nothing you don't know because I've lived like everyone else with the same mundane life, the same needs, and the same problems. We got married when I was in my fourth year at university, and we lived in Lena's room in her uncle's house. He was a career officer dismissed after 1947 and found it difficult to find a job. As a last resort, he found work in a handicraft cooperative as an assistant to the manager. To make some money during my studies, I painted watercolor cards and sold them to my colleagues on holidays or birthdays. When Uncle Vasile, Lena's uncle, who was also our godfather at the wedding, saw what I was doing, he encouraged me to work for the cooperative. They purchased all waste materials from state factories and found quality cardboard strips at a printing house from which I could cut as much as I need for my paintings. I was very happy! I could create all kinds of illustrations that people bought unframed and use like paintings in their homes. That's how

I lived until they assigned me a teacher position to a school in Videle."

"I was assigned to Videle too, in 1952" I said, nostalgically rolling through my mind the landscape of the homestead and village where I spent a summer.

"I used to come home every evening with the train from Giurgiu, which stopped at every little town. It took about two hours to reach home. Lena was pregnant and not feeling well. She constantly vomited and had dizziness and severe headaches. At first, we thought it was normal, but day by day, it was getting worse. One night, I called the ambulance. She had terrible stomach pains. I thought I was losing her. At the hospital, they found that the pregnancy was toxic and had to be terminated. Lena and I were overwhelmed with grief. She in addition to the physical pain, also suffered because she felt guilty that she couldn't give me a son. I felt helpless that I couldn't do anything to ease the depression she was going through. It was, I think, the hardest period of our lives."

"And then, did the priest find the baby?" Vali asked.

"Not really. Later, towards spring, Lena's father, the priest, lived alone because the priestess, her mother, had died of cancer several years prior. Lena was only 12 years old at the time. When the communists came to power, they sent strangers to live in people's larger houses, which exceeded 8 square meters per person. To avoid this problem, Uncle Vasile agreed with Lena's father, the priest, to let Lena stay with them because she didn't have a mother to take care of her. When the priest found the child on his steps, he didn't know what to do and ran to the church caretaker's wife, who also lived in the church courtyard, for help. Then he brought the child to us. It was a godsend that brought the light back into our home."

"I'm glad. This story was like a movie. A beautifully finished film," Vali said, getting up from the table.

"You stay longer if you want, but I'm retiring because I'm tired. But before I say good night, I want to know how the wife is?"

"She's good. As good as she can be at our age. She has arthritis, and there is humidity in our area. She suffered a lot. She wakes up at night and cries when she dreams of Angi, our little girl. What can you do when it is not in your power to change fate? May God forgive her where she is!"

"Really!" I spoke. "Come let me show you to your room."

He followed me into the guest room, where Vali prepared the bedding and what was needed for the guest. The next day, after breakfast, we parted with a promise to stay connected. He insisted on leaving one of the paintings, but we tried to convince him that his presence and stories were enough payment for our hospitality. Years have passed since then with periodic phone calls and small attentions on holidays and birthdays, but we have not had the opportunity to see each other again. Now I found out that Mrs. Gornescu decided to draft a book about Angi, their dear little girl, which helps her relive all the unique moments that united them, mother and daughter, throughout her short life.

Revenge

"Whoever says that revenge is a fool's weapon is a fool himself! Only the coward does not take revenge because that is why he is a coward. Of fear, man, of fear! You must have the courage to take revenge, and be smart. Revenge must be prepared head-on to strike where it hurts the most. So, you know! Well, you know what I did to one? Wait and see:

It was in Greece, in the refugee camp when one of our own guys came with his family and a suitcase of money; that's how the word went around the camp from someone who knew him beforehand. He had money but said he didn't have any. Let it go, is his business. But when he came here to Canada about two months after us, I went to see him at the hotel because I missed the guy. I took Zoie and the girl with me. Zoie had made hot schnitzels; I packed some beer and went to see our friends. Yes, you know I did. They were received better than we did because the government gave them paid English school. They didn't give it to us because we had Lenuța, our girl, who knew English, and we could manage with her. After that, I said: Let me take him with me to the hotel where I worked, because these Canadiens fools who wondered there are up to no good. I talked to the boss, and he hired him. He put us both on the evening shift when there was less work, and we could chat until midnight. We didn't really have anything else to do. It was good!

When someone called with a problem, we went together, and the guy didn't give up because he was handy and hardworking. After that, we would go to report that everything was fine, and we would go back to our workshop to chat.

One day, the guy comes to work with a brand-new car, a limousine, sir, a Chevrolet Impala. I knew he wanted to get a car, but I thought he wanted a used one for the occasion. I said:

"Okay, cousin, you with the new car and me with my rabble that I took you to Niagara?"

"Leave it, brother; I took it in installments. You can do the same."

"Well, to take it in installments, I need money for the down payment. No?"

"I'll give it to you. You give it back to me when you can."

Said and done. He gave me $1500, and I got a Ford Marquise, better than his. When I first came with it to the hotel, the boss and those from the morning shift widened their eyes; they could not believe it. We, the immigrants with new cars, and they, the English, with their rabble. That is right!

"Then why did you take revenge on him?"

"Well, wait and see, the story didn't end there... He said he was some kind of engineer in I don't know what, and that he found an evening class at George Brown College where he wanted to go. He moved to the morning shift, and I was left alone in the evening. After about two days, when I met him at lunch, he told me that the boss asked him to organize the workshop. Another two days passed, and I saw in the corridor outside of the workshop solid wood panels and angle-shaped metal bars perforated with holes all along their length. Before, I used to sit in the workshop in front of my desk, but after that, I didn't even have a place anymore. He began to put these metal shelves on legs tightly tightened around the walls. Where there were no shelves, he installed wooden panels with hooks to hang various tools. Then instead of the desk I used to sit at because I also had the phone installed on it, there appeared a solid workbench, vises anchored in screws to the thick wooden headboard, and down under, another shelf for boxes or other things. So now, instead of the desk where I could sit comfortably, I got this bench. When the phone rang, I had to stand up. The boss grew with pride and happiness because of what he had achieved. When everything was ready, he called the management to see what he had done. It's true that everything looked different now. When the chief accountant found out about the changes done in our workshop, he asked for shelves like these to be made for him because you see, all his files were buried in boxes stacked on top of each other, and it was a problem to find what he needed. When he finished his job here, everyone spoke about my friend. The whole story started to bother me. I started to look for work in other places because if I didn't have anything to do in the workshop, I would not want to spend time there.

At the reception desk in the main hall, worked a beautiful doll. She had that sweet smile that held you in place. One evening, when I went there to talk with her, she was friendly and not shy about a compliment or a joke. Then she asked me where my friend was. I told her that he worked mornings. After about two days, I did not see her anymore. I asked and found out that she switched to the morning shift. Beautiful, I said to myself...

After that, it was before Christmas; it snowed so hard that it was barely possible to drive. When I arrived at the hotel parking lot, I saw the girl at the reception with my friend. They both got into his car.

"That's the way it goes," I say to myself, "and the bandit hasn't said a word about it."

I took him aside the next day and said,

"Are you successful with young girls, Don Juan?"

"What girls? You mean the colleague at the reception desk?"

"Colleague, what are you calling her now? I see, you know."

"Yes. She has her child in kindergarten, and she is always late if she takes the bus. It is on my way. I take her there."

"I was just joking. I know that you are a serious guy."

I said to myself, breaking away from him: "Let's say I got a cure for you, too." After a few days, I came early and went straight to the reception desk in the hotel lobby. She was there.

"What's new? I haven't seen you in a long time," I said.

"Yes. I changed to the morning shift."

"Oh! It's so sad in the evening when I work, and you're not there. I don't even have anyone to talk to."...

"Let's say you'll find someone for a compliment."...

"No, seriously now. I came early, especially to tell you something, but it must remain a secret. I heard from the boys in the shop that my friend, you know who is the one who drives you. He says he managed to seduce you. I think he dreams about you. If his wife finds out, I do not know how you will feel. And then the children"...

"That's unbelievable! I did not even imagine. Say no more, please! I don't want to listen to anything else anymore! Good thing you told me! That's it! Goodbye." And she left with tears in her eyes.

"OK! I arranged it," I told myself.

I unlocked the door of a room facing the parking lot and saw my friend waiting for the girl from reception.

"Wait for her, dear boy; she'll come when you'll see the back of your neck!"

Also, during that period, the boss had a meeting with management. When done, he came over to me in the shop.

"How's it going? Is everything OK?"

"No problem," I said. "How was the meeting?"

"Better for us than other departments. Only a few complaints with the electrical installation and the bathrooms that the showers don't work like they should."

"You know, boss. I think you should pay more attention to what people say."

"What are people saying?"

"Hey, can't you see that dude does it all by himself? People don't even come to you anymore when they have a problem. They go to him directly. Is he telling you what he did? No. Do you know he is an engineer? Now he goes to school here. Everyone knows that he can fix everything. I would be more careful."

The boss didn't say anything. He shook my hand in silence and walked away from me thoughtfully. It was about a week before I saw my friend. He was happy to see me:

"I have news that will surprise you. I saw a great apartment in a nice block with security at the entrance and other wonderful things. I made an offer to buy it.

"What are you talking about? Aren't you afraid? What if you lose your job?"

"I'll be finding another now that I have Canadian experience. I also could have good references from the hotel. I don't think it is a problem. And then do the math: the money you pay for rent goes away. You have nothing in exchange. If you buy an apartment, the principal is deducted from the debt, so you earn it. Speaking of which, I think I'm going to need the money I loaned you for the car."

"Well, didn't you say I'd give it back to you when I could?"

"I did, but then I didn't know I would need it now."

"Let us see until then. Come on, does the girl from reception still come with you every day?"

"No. I do not know what's wrong with her; she doesn't even answer my greeting. I wanted to ask, and she turned her back on me. So do others in her office. Their business, I have no idea."

"I'll inquire and let you know. What other projects does the boss have for you?"

"None. More recently, he sent me to sweep the front entrance of the hotel every morning. He told me to report to him when someone asked me to fix something, but he did not send me there to fix the problem. He's been acting a bit strange too."

"What are you saying? I'm so sorry!"

Inwardly, I was jubilant. But that was not all. He wanted me to give him his money back.

"I will pay it," I said to myself, "with interest!"

So, I did. The boss started visiting me more often when I was alone on duty. He was coming to spy on me. I pretended to be worried and advised him to act in such a way as to make him leave the hotel on his own. I told him to complain to the management about the guy being insubordinate and not following orders. Make a written report and bring a witness, if possible. The boss listened attentively to every word. When he put my friend on the evening shift again, the friend protested and went to the union with a complaint. That hastened his sentence. They kicked him out. When he came to work on Easter Friday, the boss handed him the envelope with the pink dismissal paper. In the same envelope was the money from me, the 1500 dollars he gave me. That was the coup de grace. He was supposed to move into the new apartment on May 1st, but he did not have a job now.

That is why I say revenge is not a fool's weapon."

"And what else do you know about him? Did he manage?"

"I found out that he was employed by a Romanian who had a furniture factory, but he didn't stay there long either. Then he went to a big car company. He became chief engineer there; I think he still works there. Earns well. He got a new house with a big yard and a two-car garage. But I never saw him again. The guy was not stupid. He knew what he was doing."

"From what I can see, you did him a favor. If you did nothing, he would still be working at the hotel today and would not have the money for a new house. Aren't you sorry for what you did to him?"

"Why should I be sorry? It ruined all my aims. Because of him, no one saw me with good eyes either. I was fired because a housekeeper whom I tried to kiss complained. It was a big mess. Since then, my daughter doesn't talk to me either. That's life, sir! One day sunny, one day cold, one day heaven, one day walled!"

Diana

When my son met Diana, the niece brought from Romania by our neighbor from the penthouse, we were happy that he had found a friend from our homeland. I believe they met in the building's elevator, probably hearing her speak Romanian to someone on the phone. I found out this story one day at dinner when my wife, curious, wanted to know more about her while grilling Costin with questions. Otherwise, we, the ones living on the fifth floor of a building with over 20 floors, had no way of knowing who lived in the penthouse, whether they were Romanian or not. At my wife Mariana's suggestion, Costin brought Diana over one day. From then on, she began to visit more often. She was pretty, friendly, and cheerful and brought with her a fresh, spring-like vibe. She grew close to Mariana, who became quite fond of her. She couldn't have been more than 20 or 21 years old; she understood English but struggled to speak it, which made it difficult for her to work. Her uncle apparently had a good job with the government or a government enterprise. He was almost always away, often for days on end. Since he was unmarried, when Diana felt lonely, he would come over to our place.

Costin treated her like an older brother. He would sometimes take her to his friends, to the movies, or show her around the city. Mariana and I were happy with this arrangement, as we liked the girl, and she seemed to be a good match for him in both age and appearance. Thus, Costin's summer vacation at home passed. Before Labour Day, he decided to take his things to his apartment in Waterloo, where he had been living for many years. Diana asked if she could join him on this day trip, and Costin, who was pleased not to make the trip alone, agreed. About two days after they returned from Waterloo, Diana didn't visit, but then she invited us to her uncle's penthouse apartment the following day, right before the weekend. Costin had been there before, but we had not.

Mariana went to buy flowers for Diana, and at the appointed time, we went to her place. Her uncle was at a conference abroad, and no one else was there except for us. Diana greeted us joyfully in a long, colorful floral dress that suited her beautifully, with her loose hair covering her shoulders, appearing from the wide neckline that partially revealed the delicate curves of her breasts. Mariana and I were impressed by the spacious apartment, the fine, classic-style furniture, the library, the paintings, and the carpets that seemed too precious to step on. There was also a terrace from which you could admire the city. The table filled with all kinds of delicacies prepared by Diana, including fine porcelain plates, silverware, and crystal, awaited us in the dining room. It was a remarkably beautiful day, during which Diana excelled as a hostess, serving us gracefully, politely declining Mariana's offer to help, and at the same time, engaging in amusing conversation with each of us. After dessert and coffee, Mariana and I returned home, and Costin stayed a little longer to help her clean up.

After Costin returned to university, life resumed at a normal, quieter pace, with fewer phone calls and pop music vibrating through the house. Diana also started visiting less often. One day, she told Mariana that she had received a phone call from a former boyfriend from Romania, who had recently arrived in Canada, and that she really wanted to see him. Mariana wasn't curious to know more about this friend, and Diana didn't say anything else about him. The matter was soon forgotten until one day!

About a week had passed since Diana had last visited. This was a bit odd, but we didn't think it was our place to ask questions, although Diana had earned a special place in our family. We missed her, and Mariana was feeling guilty, thinking she might have said something to upset her. We waited to see what would happen. I had just come home one evening, and while Mariana was preparing dinner, the phone rang. I answered:

"Hello, the Preda family?"

"Yes."

"My wife, Diana, is she at your place?"

"Your wife or your niece?" I asked the man on the other end of the line.

"My wife. Diana, my wife."

At this declaration, I almost dropped the receiver.

"I'm sorry, who am I speaking to?"

"I'm your neighbor from the penthouse. My name is Vasile Cojocaru. I found your phone number on our agenda, and I knew you were friends. I just got back from a work trip today, and I can't find her at home… So, I'm asking if she's with you?"

"No, she's not here. We haven't seen her in a few days."

"Then where is she?"

At that question, I was stunned. Mariana, who had been listening to my conversation, froze upon hearing what had been said.

"Do you know anything about Diana?" I asked her, covering the mouthpiece. She shook her head no.

"Mr. Cojocaru, we're sorry, but we don't know anything. We'll call our son at university. Maybe he knows something about Diana."

"Then please let me know what you find out."

"Certainly! We'll call you after we speak with him."

"Thank you."

"You're welcome," I said, placing the phone down.

Mariana and I remained silent, looking at each other. We suspected that our son was in love with Diana, just like we were. For that reason, we didn't know how to tell him without causing him pain. Any deception brings suffering. How could Diana do something so unforgivable? Why did she deceive us all? We found no answers. We waited a little longer, and after dinner, Mariana picked up the phone and called our son. Costin answered, and after a few words, she asked him what he knew about Diana.

"I don't know anything except what she told me when she came with me to Waterloo."

"What did she say then?"

"That she was unhappy. She said she wanted to return to Romania. She said she felt lonely here and had no prospects."

"And what did you say to her?"

"I told her she was wrong! She had us. If she waited a little longer until I'll finish and get my diploma, I would ask her uncle for her hand in marriage."

"And what did she say?"

Costin didn't answer immediately. After a pause, he told Mariana that things were complicated and unclear. There was more to the story with Diana.

"In what way?" asked Mariana.

"I don't know either. She mentioned going back to Romania when we were returning home from Waterloo. When I said I'd ask her to marry me, she hesitated. 'What's wrong?' I asked. 'Don't you want me as your husband?' She didn't answer. She turned her head toward the window next to her and stayed like that, looking out. When we parked the car at home, I held her by the shoulders; I think I wanted to kiss her. She pulled back and said, 'Not here. Come upstairs to my place.' In the apartment, she sat on the couch in the living room and told me without looking at me that she wasn't going to marry me. 'Why?' I asked. 'Don't you love me?' No answer. She remained silent, staring at the carpet. I held her and kissed her face. She didn't resist. I lifted her chin and kissed her lips, her eyes, her forehead, her neck, and she didn't react at all. Not even when I touched her breasts or unbuttoned her blouse she didn't resist. She was so soft, like a rag doll with which I could do anything. I stood up then and went home. I don't even know if I ate anything that evening. I was upset hurt, and my pride was shattered, as if I wasn't myself anymore. It was that she invited us over to her place. I stayed there after you left, remember? I wanted to help her. I thought maybe I'd find out what was going on, why she was refusing to be my wife, and how she was acting the way she did. After she walked you to the door after dinner, she told me she didn't want to clear the table just yet. She came up to me, very close, unzipped the back of her dress, letting it fall to the floor, and her bare body stood there in front of me. Then she threw herself into my arms: 'You know I love you; you fool! But I can't be your wife. I'm yours! Always yours! Now ease my longing for you, and don't ask me why!' she said, kissing me like a thirsty animal. Then she took me by the hand and led me to the bedroom in front of the bed. She was a different person, completely unrecognizable."

"She didn't tell you she was married?"

"Married? Her? To whom?"

"To her uncle!"

"That's impossible…"

"It is possible! He called today to ask where his wife was."

"I did not know anything. I called her and left messages, but she did not respond."

"When did you last speak to her?"

"Before I went back to Waterloo when I went to say goodbye. She was waiting for me at her place…"

"And you haven't heard anything since?"

"No!"

After the conversation with him, I called Mr. Cojocaru back to tell him that Costin didn't know anything about Diana except that she had told him she wanted to return to Romania.

"I knew this would happen," said Mr. Cojocaru after a moment of reflection.

"You see, I am 30 years older than she is. But she and her mother, a past time colleague from the Romanian Department of Extern Commerce, insisted on bringing her to Canada, and as there was no better solution to accelerate the process, I married her. I do not regret it! It was a dream. A short but beautiful dream."

Corina

Well, when I was released from the army in '54 at the age of twenty, Corina would have been less than 30 at the time. She was staying in our courtyard with her mother and her husband, a supervisor at the Armătura, a small metallurgical enterprise located on the western side of the Basarab bridge, not far from the cigarette factory. He, nenea Ștefan (Uncle Stephan, this is how we used to call the older), also took me there to work as a technician during vacations. He was an industrious, capable man and well-regarded by all at the company. But living with his mother-in-law, who came in visit from Brăila, an eastern side city, and remained with them ever since, led him one day to say sorry and never return home again. After the pronouncement of the divorce, the mother and daughter began to look through acquaintances for a man to support them because neither one nor the other had ever worked. It is true that the old woman had a pension from her deceased husband, but with that, she could barely pay the bills for the house she had in Brăila. Here, however, although the rent was not high, it had to be paid on time as the owner, Mr. Moldoveanu, did not allow past-due payments.

Finally, they found what they were looking for. The man, an accountant by trade, was in his late fifties and had a shrapnel scar on his forehead, which brought his mouth closer to his right ear. It wasn't easy to like him because he was arrogant, unpleasant with his neighbors, and always had objections at paying the common expenses. Soon after moving into our yard, the mother-in-law had to return home to Brăila because the son-in-law was not willing to care for two people. It's said that soon after this event, the old woman ended up in solitude and was found dead by neighbors. All this happened before I returned home from the army.

I start smoking in the army, and my parents always insisted that I give up cigarettes. In the evening, after the heat of the summer days, I would go outside to smoke on the bench under the open kitchen windows. Corina often sat next to me because smoking gave a lady more distinction. In her dreamy eyes, she was sad that she had not been lucky enough to have a romantic love, as she read in novels. Sometimes, she would tell me about how she had been solicited by many admirers in her youth but was unlucky because of the war, the refuge of her hometown due to the war, and the envy of other girls who stole her suitors by doing them favors that she, a good girl, would not do for them. She married Stefan because he was a good match, a settled man with a furnished house, but she never loved him. Because of that, she had never considered having children with him. She kept thinking that one day, she would meet her true love, and then everything would be different.

"But now, the marriage with the one-eyed guy," she said, "you know, his right eye is made of glass, it's a misalliance."

Corina's confession in a whisper one evening surprised me, knowing that he was taking his siesta in the living room, flipping through the newspaper. I had not yet had the opportunity to meet women disappointed in their marriages, and Corina, with her confidential air in which she poured all her intimate thoughts, ignited in me a kind of erotic feeling as she sat next to me on the bench in the courtyard. She looked like a ripe fruit that tempted one to bite. At the time, although the temptation instigated me to hold her in my arms, the thought of committing an act that would end these moments of closeness and the fear that other neighbors may see stopped me from risking any gesture.

Often, she encouraged me to tell her about my love affairs, but at the time, my experience lacked the flavor of romance she pursued because the only love that kept me company throughout my military service ended when I came home. My girlfriend confessed to me that she loved someone else. As she listened to my story, Corina became even closer to me. She tried to ease my heart from the burden of disappointment with caresses and whispers full of secret understanding and gave me hope that true love would dawn on the horizon.

Towards the end of the summer, an unforeseen fact changed the situation: One night, a car stopped in the street in front of the court, and two agents lifted the poor husband out of bed, as he was in his pajamas, leaving behind a mess in the rummaged and devastated home. The next day, upon learning what happened, each of us, stunned by the news, did not know what to believe. Corina didn't leave the house for two days out of anger and shame. No one knew why he was arrested and what the police wanted to find in their house. Shortly after Christmas, Corina received notification that her husband was tried for fraud and sentenced to years of prison.

One day, she met me shopping at Alimentara, a dairy market:

"Why are you avoiding me?"

"I'm not avoiding you, but it's cold, and I don't go outside to smoke anymore," I stammered.

"Why don't you come to see me? Are you as the others who can't even bother to say hello? I thought you were my friend, my only friend…" she said.

"How could I come? What would my family and neighbors say?"

"The hell with everyone! Here is what I want you to do for me: I want you to make a phone call to this number. Say that you know someone who has a room for rent. See what they say, take all the information and give them my address. Do you understand?"

"And what can I say about the rent?"

"That you do not negotiate this matter. They need to talk to me."

"Why don't you answer the phone?"

"I don't know the person. I want first to know if they are male or female... Do you understand? Try to find out as many details as possible to be prepared."

"How can I tell you?"

"I'll see you tomorrow in the lobby at the Marna cinema. Seven o'clock, but don't be late! There is a good movie."

The next day, I went to the movie, and for the first time, I put my arm around her shoulders, but she did not allow me more than that.

"Why won't you let me kiss you?"

"Not here! People will see us."

"How can they see us? It's dark?"

"No! Be good!"

On the way back home, I told her what I had discussed on the phone with the person in question. The guy was a watchmaker who worked privately from home. He had many connections and made a living from services for those who did not know how to manage the complicated problems of time. He knew a young woman in the country who wanted a legitimate address in Bucharest, hard to obtain. He also found her a job at Alpaca, a clothing factory. Corina had to guarantee her a stable residence to let the girl obtain a

Bucharest visa.

"Did you give him my address?" asked Corina.

"He said he could not come to you. You must go to him. I have his address in my pocket."

"Will you come with me there tomorrow?"

"Maybe," I told her, smiling."

When we arrived home, our courtyard was covered by darkness. I led Corina on tiptoe to her front door and opened it; before turning on the light, we slipped inside. I grabbed her by the shoulders in the dark, and with her back against the wall, I pulled the hood off her head and tried to kiss her. But she turned her head away. Then I grasped her waist through the opening of her coat. Corina found the moment to resolutely push me out.

"Be good. I'm tired now. Go home," she told me.

"Why don't you want me to sleep here? You know how much I want you."

"No! I'm tired! Good night!" and she opened the door and pushed me out.

I didn't insist. Her opposition was imperative, leaving no room for negotiation, so I went home sullen, defeated, and confused. I felt her so close, warm, and encouraging at certain moments and, at the same time, distant whenever I got closer to her. I desired her, but I didn't know what to do. The next day, I went with her to the watchmaker's home, but I paid no attention to the discussion between them. On returning home, I did not try to enter her apartment again. She saw from my monosyllabic answers that I was upset but didn't try to find out why. We didn't see each other again for the rest of the week.

Sunday evening, a horse-driven car stopped in front of the gate, and a young woman got out carrying a trunk helped by an older man. They entered Corina's home. The man carried a few more bags from the car into the house, and after a while, he climbed back into the car and left. Corina's tenant was gone most of the day, even on Sunday. I found out several days later from Corina when I met her at the tobacco shop on the corner. Nela, the girl who lived with her, was an activist of the communist youth union and the actions she organized, kept her busy all day. But she was a good girl; she paid the rent on time, and her father brought flour, cornmeal, potatoes, and everything else from the countryside.

"And what do you do alone all day?" I asked, trying to move the conversation to another topic.

"What to do? I cook, clean, read a little, and wait until Nela comes so we can exchange a few more words together."

"Aren't we friends? Didn't you say that you have only me?"

"Yes, but how? What you want cannot happen to me. That's

all I need to entertain the gossip people..."

"What are you doing now? Let's go to a movie."

"I can't. I'm not dressed."

"You are fine the way you are. Are you coming with me?"

"Are you crazy? How am I going to come like this? Tomorrow at six, at Marna!" and with that, she left me alone in the middle of the street.

We entered the balcony in the dark, on one of the last rows. There was no one behind us, and after placing our coats on our knees, I put my arm around her shoulders, pulling her closer to me. She was looking intently at the screen but let herself lean against my chest, feeling her breath. She was warm, soft, and malleable, like dough. Keeping my hand under her arm, I could feel her bust with all its curves in my palm. Never has she been so close to me; I wanted time to stand still. Never have I wanted a woman as much as I wanted Corina that evening. But the movie ended, the lights came on in the hall, and as the hall emptied of spectators, a few of them, like us, were waiting for the resumption of the movie. After a ten-minute pause, when it was dark again, I slipped my hand under our overcoats to find her knees. Her black dress, slightly pulled up, let me feel the smooth touch of the silk stocking beneath my fingers. But just above the knee, the stocking came under the elastic grip of a pair of flannel cotton knickers that stopped any research intent:

"Didn't you find something else to wear?" I asked.

"In this cold?"

Resigned, I retreated to my chair. After the movie, we went to a pastry shop. I ordered two savarins with a grand dome of whipped cream built over a syrupy scone base. They were delicious. Corina was also delicious. Her eyes shone, her teeth glistened, bared with every smile, and I, haunted by what had happened so far, felt like a besieger in front of a capitulated fortress with all the gates open, unable to find the entrance. When we got close to the house, she told me that we were parting there.

"You enter the courtyard five minutes after me," she said.

"Will you leave the lights off and the door open so I can come too?"

"No. Nela must come now."

"When will I see you again?"

"I don't know," and she left me again.

Several weeks passed. I met a girl I liked at work, and I started seeing her. She had just finished high school and was staying with her parents, and after they met me, they allowed us to go out together but not to bring her home late. When I returned home one evening, in front of our gate, a large car, a limousine, was stationed. Nela, accompanied by a well-dressed man, entered Corina's home.

The limousine and driver were waiting at the gate. Later, after I finished eating, I went outside to smoke. The limousine was still at the gate, and from Corina's apartment, there was talk, laughter, music, and the clinking of crystal. After that, the limousine at our gate became a regular occurrence. Nela's friend was, it seems, a man who equally enjoyed Nela's friendship and Corina's gourmet dishes. He came often, even when Nela was not at home.

Until a day: It was raining; one rainy day of spring supposed to remove the last remaining patches of snow from winter. The limousine was back in front of the gate when Nela came rushing in with a wet trench coat on her. As soon as she closed the door behind her, women screamed as if the house was on fire. Moments later, they were out in the middle of the yard, Nela pulling Corina by the hair like a horned vine under the torrential rain of water, swearing:

"You, miserable whore! Can't you get enough? Are you looking for my man now? A parasite, that's what you are, sucking the life of the workers. Let me teach you, bitch! I teach you what work means! You will see!"

Corina was struggling, screaming in pain, and when Nela let her go, she collapsed on the wet pavement like a sack of potatoes. She had bare feet, and all her clothing was a satin shirt that only partially covered her body. After Nela entered the house, Corina rushed to the door to follow her in, but found it locked. Kneeling on the entrance step, battered by the freezing rain, Corina buried her face in her hands, crying to those inside her house to let her in, too. Her prayers went unanswered. Then my mother went to pick her up from the floor, bringing her into our kitchen. She was wet as if she had just stepped out of the shower. The thin shirt had become as transparent as a sheet of cellophane, and she was trying to cover her breasts and the black spot of her thighs with her palms. Mother brought a blanket from the bedroom and wrapped it around her. She poured hot water from the teapot on the stove into two cups and gave her a cup to warm herself up. Corina, crouched by the fire, continued to cry, clutching the teacup with one hand as if she wanted to warm her fingers. With her head bowed so that we could not see her face, she began to speak:

"It was a plan, I think; I didn't realize it at first. When I let that man into the house, I considered him a friend and a guest: I treated him to coffee and cake and had a civilized conversation with him. Then he started telling me how attracted he was to me and complimented me. Then he came up to me, took me in his arms, started kissing me, and while I was fighting him, he pulled off the robe I was wearing and threw me on the bed. I struggled, I begged him, I cried, but he didn't hear anything. He pounced on me like a monster and raped me. I didn't have the strength to fight him." Corina, exhausted, paused, then looking my mother in the eye, she said:

"After he raped me, I wanted to get up, wash myself, clean off every trace of this animal touch, but he wouldn't let me. He continued to lay over me, holding me firmly under his body as if he knew something was about to happen. And indeed, after a little while, when I was almost numb under his weight, Nela walked in on us. She beat me, pulled my hair, and threw me out of the house. From my house and my things," and she started to cry again.

"Mother… If my mother had been by my side, none of this would have happened. She would know how to avoid them; she was wise. What should I do now? Where should I go? They kicked me out of my house, and I have no one to help me," she continued through tears.

To calm her down, my mother motioned for me to leave her alone in the kitchen to let her collect her thoughts. She was full of pity for this young woman and understood that she had to help her somehow. She took out a dress of hers from the wardrobe, a pair of shoes, and stockings and brought them to her. She asked her if she was hungry, but Corina refused. By now, it was getting dark outside, and the limousine at the gate was no longer there either. While my mother was thinking about where to put Corina to bed in our two-room cottage, we heard a knock on the door, and I went to open it. There were two police officers:

"Is citizen Corina here?"

Mother appeared at the door:

"But what happened?"

"Citizen Corina must come with us. She's accused of parasitism and pimping."

"Yes, but she could be innocent, a victim, in fact."

"You mind your own business; you're not a lawyer! The citizen must come with us; that's the law!"

Corina gathered her last shred of dignity and walked out of the kitchen straight, silent, and without a word, hugged my mother and me, and left with them. I never heard from her again.

Nicu, Mara, Vali and Me

If I had known what was going to happen, I probably wouldn't have gone there. Definitely not. But now it's too late: the dice were cast, and nothing could change. It all started with a trivial event, a twist of fate: Nicu and I were at the pond, roasting in the sun. Behind us, a noisy group of young people, boys, and girls, found a shadier spot under the canopy of a wild tree and settled on mats and towels, ready to dive into the mirror-like surface of the water. There were others around, too, but we didn't pay attention to them. I was smoking calmly, watching the athletic silhouette of a blonde girl walking by on her way to the lake. She was tall, with fair skin, about the height of Yolanda Balaș, our high jump champion, and like her, dressed in a one-piece black swimsuit. My friend, a giant nearly two meters tall, also blond and a real ladies' man, nudged me with his elbow:

"That chick is hot! Don't you want to pick her up?"

"Now? I have such a laziness it could touch the sky!"

"Your call. I'm going!"

"Go ahead," I said, stretching out face down on the sandy shore with patches of grass here and there.

The group of young people under the tree gathered in a circle around a boy who began tuning the strings of a guitar, encouraged by the girls to play something. One of them, with her hair tied in a bun and sunburned skin, looked familiar to me, although I had never spoken to her. She was the girl I often saw crossing Grant Bridge, which meant we lived in the same neighborhood. The boy with the guitar started singing one of the Italian songs introduced to us by the singer Giani Spinelli and overwhelmed by the heat of the sun; I closed my eyes. I must have dozed off because I saw myself floating in a boat, my head resting on the floral blue skirt of Paula, the girl I had recently met but hadn't yet confessed my love to her. She leaned over my head, so close that I wanted to wrap my arms around her neck to kiss her. Then suddenly, Paula jumped up, horrified:

"Where did the blond guy go?"

"Which blond?" I asked, jumping to my feet.

"The tall guy who went into the lake." The answer came from the girl from Grant Bridge.

"And what happened?"

"I don't know; we stayed here on the shore. But Mara, our friend whom he was following, dove under and quickly came back to us. He didn't surface again."

"Did he dive, too?"

"I don't know. I wasn't watching."

"And the others in the group?"

"No one knows."

"Not even Mara?"

"No, she ran away from him."

I didn't know what to think. The whole group of young people under the tree was now behind me, watching to see what I would do. Stunned by the news of his sudden disappearance, I couldn't think of anything, as if struck by lightning. "How could he just disappear like that?" I asked myself.

"Maybe he's hiding behind some bushes on the shore out of embarrassment?" I suggested. Some of the young people seemed to agree with my guess, so I asked:

"Who will help me search around?"

Several volunteers followed me into the water. We swam to both sides of the lake, Nicu's name, my missing friend, echoing from many voices across the water's surface, but no trace. There were no signs to confirm he had been there. When evening came, we decided to go as a group to the local police station. Mara, the blonde girl who resembled Yolanda Balaș, was crying, full of remorse for not being more friendly to Nicu, who had only wanted to know her name:

"Why won't you tell me your name? Look, I'm Nicu. I want us to be friends." That's all he said, and now look what had happened, the girl kept repeating, wiping her tears with the back of her hands.

With the help of others, I gathered Nicu's clothes into a small bundle and took them with us. At the police station, we were each asked to write a statement about what we knew, but I was questioned by an officer who wanted information about Nicu. I told him everything I knew, and then we were allowed to go home. The officer assured us that a team of divers would be sent to search the lake's bottom. We parted ways on the street, each of us shaken by the inexplicable sorrow of Nicu's disappearance, a remarkable young man, both physically and full of life.

The girl from Grant Bridge walked with me on the way home. We were both sad, consumed by the event, and had little to discuss. Passing through the park, we sat on a bench.

"Were you two close?" she broke the silence.

"Not really, just colleagues. We worked together."

"How do you explain what happened today?"

"That's the thing, I can't explain it at all. He had an instinct for pretty girls, but he wasn't aggressive or trying to take advantage of them. I don't know how likable he was; I'm not a girl... He asked me to go into the water with him, and I regret not going. I was too lazy..."

"I understand. You're not to blame; don't feel guilty... Was he sick? Did he have heart problems?"

"I don't know! He never mentioned it."

"I had a friend. Her brother, Nae, as we called him, was a great athlete on the national swim team. Young, handsome like an Adonis. He died suddenly after a competition. The effort was too much. That's why I'm asking."

"What's your name?" she asked after a while, noticing I hadn't responded.

"Doru. Actually, it's Tudor, but people call me Doru."

"I'm Valentina, but everyone calls me Vali. Do you have any siblings?"

"A sister."

"Is she blonde, blue-eyed, and freckled?"

"Yes."

"I think I know her. I've seen her with some friends. She's very pretty..."

"It runs in the family," I said, smiling.

"Not you... I think you were made by another mother," Vali joked, laughing.

"Is that how you see me? Ugly?"

"No. I'm kidding. Let's go..."

I walked with her to the gate of her family's house. But we kept talking until late that night. I hadn't noticed how quickly time had passed. We agreed to meet the next day after work; maybe we'd find out more about Nicu.

The next day at lunch break, someone tapped me on the shoulder. I turned around, and there was Nicu, just as tall as before and with the same mischievous smile. I couldn't believe my eyes after all the fear from the previous day. It was like seeing a ghost:

"What's with you? We thought you were dead yesterday..."

"What's with me? I got lost from you guys and ended up on the road."

"How did you get lost? You were right in front of us."

"When I dove after that blonde girl, I hit my head on something hard, concrete or some heavy solid object; I don't know because I don't remember what happened next. I flailed around as much as I could, and when I finally surfaced, I was in some reeds and didn't know how to get out to reach the shore. I walked a bit, reached the bridge, and saw the road. A truck passed by and stopped, and the guy, an honest fellow, gave me a ride home."

"We went to the police and reported you dead..."

"I know. They came to my house to notify my parents. I told

them what happened too. They said they'll investigate the spot where I hit my head... They mentioned that unexploded bombs from the war had been found in that area before; there might be one buried in the mud at the bottom of the lake... Where are my clothes?" Nicu asked, referring to the clothes left on the shore of the pond.

"Didn't you get them? I left them at the police station..."

"No problem. I'll go there after work..."

That's pretty much Nicu's story. When I told Vali in the evening about his reappearance, I couldn't convince her to wait until the next day to inform her group, especially Mara, the girl who resembled Yolanda Balaş. So, we went straight to her. Mara asked me to go with her to Nicu's house because she wanted to talk to him. It's hard to get the last word with these girls, so I went with them. They got married before Christmas, and Vali and I were guests of honor. We didn't waste time either; in the spring, we had a big wedding. It's been 60 years since then...

Fidelity

One of my wife's acquaintances told her a confidential secret about a mutual friend, Olga, whom we know from our group of friends that we often gather out with. Olga and Puiu had been together for several years, but she had started to get bored with his long, overly detailed complains about problems he has with colleagues and bosses at work. When they had guests, whether they were family or not, Puiu would start repeating the same stories that, after a while, started to exasperate her. She knew that Puiu was a good, diligent man and that he cared about her, but the fact that he had to bear his soul to everyone was too much for her, and feeling embarrassed, she started pretending to listen when her mind was elsewhere.

She had problems, too, but she didn't tell anyone about them. She tried to hide them even from herself. Money was scarce, their accumulated earnings barely covered their daily needs, and it was not easy having a small child to take to daycare every day. But who could she talk to about what she was going through, and what good would it do to complain to others about her hardships? She had more problems that she could counter. At work, where she was a telephone operator at the headquarters of a large company, some colleagues and bosses tried to seduce her with advances. The envy and gossip of other colleagues forcing her to put up being new to this place, kept quiet as she didn't want to cause problems. But what she got to listen to daily on the headset connecting phone calls, made her blush. Coming from a family of simple people, but with common sense and a dose of faith in the holy Bible, she was shocked seeing her colleagues, married and with children, allowing themselves to go out during breaks with foreign men who courted them. She wasn't spying on them, but she could hear them chatting with other female colleagues about what they had done and where they had been. All these things made her think, "How could they be so disloyal? Why do they do this? For money, or for pleasure?" Like a good observer, she waited silently to see what would happen next.

To be honest, I didn't have a particular attraction for Olga. Although she had blue eyes like the sky, blond hair, and a tiny ant's waist, I did not like the way she behaved with Puiu, who, every time he would start to tell his stories, intervened rather brutally, saying: "You repeat yourself, dear. You've said this once or twice!" He would get angry in silence, but at the first opportunity, he would snap like a matchstick, and it wasn't unusual to have a face-to-face argument with everyone around.

Rather, Crina, with her dimples on her cheeks and a permanent smile on her lips, is another friend of my wife married to Gica. I can say it gave me more pleasure. This one, younger than me by about ten years, had more charm, was funny, voluble, knew how to say interesting things, and gave the impression that she admired her husband. Gica was an appreciate engineer at a large international company, and since she had married him, she liked to share his title as Mrs. Engineer so and so, even though she was a nurse at a hospital.

In our group were other couples who we would meet at small gatherings on weekends. We used to go out together to picnics in the summer, shows, restaurants, or just to play cards. The women separated from the men after the meal was served, eager to find out what the world was saying. The men, around the table over a cigarette and a glass of wine, would talk politics, play a game of poker, or both at the same time. When we got home, Luiza, my wife, would start saying:

"Do you know what Elena told me?"

"Who is Elena? The one with short hair, glasses, and married to the university professor?"

"No, that's Zoe. She calls herself madam professor Zoe as if we don't know that she was his secretary years ago before he left his wife. Elena is married to Dr. Pitaru. She told me that - but this is a secret, you know - that the guy brought by Olga and Puiu tonight, Nicu, is not, as they introduced him, a friend; he is their tenant. He rented a room in Olga's house after he separated from his wife."

"What are you talking about dear?"

"Yes, but Elena found out about this from her seamstress, whom she has known for many years and lives across from Olga's house. The guy works from home, and his car is parked in front of the house. Did you see how he looked at each of us? And he didn't talk much."

"Yes, he seems like an interesting guy."

"And I found out something else: A woman comes to his place sometimes to clean. But what cleaning did she have to do in one room? Olga thought she was his mistress."

"Um! Interesting."

"Yes. One day, she told the guy that she didn't allow other women into her house. She asked him to tell the woman not to come again. He didn't get mad but said he needed someone to clean, that he wasn't good at it. Then Olga offered to do this job because no one knows the house better than her, but she won't do it for free."

"How do you know all this?" I asked.

"Well, don't you understand? From Elena, who goes to the seamstress. And Olga goes to her too. That's why any time she comes to a party, she wears a new dress. You saw how the others came dressed. This seamstress knows how to combine an old dress with something new, and suddenly, a new dress appears. I think I'll go to her too, especially since she doesn't cost a lot."

"And Olga discusses with her what is happening at her house?"

"Well, if they are neighbors... That seamstress sees everything."

Not long after, Gica, the engineer, received a job in a facility under construction in Texas and had to work there. Every six months, the company allows the spouses to spend a week of vacation together, either at home with the whole family or at work if he's in the middle of an urgent project. Crina couldn't wait to go to Houston, where Gica worked, but Gica told her on the phone that it was better not to come there this time.

"Why? Are you coming home?"

"No, I'm not coming. I have too much work."

"Then why don't I come to you?"

"Because you can't. It's a mess."

"What kind of mess? Are you caught up in the mess?"

"Yes!"

"With a woman?"

"Yes."

"How can you do such a thing? You leave me here with two kids, and you…"

"I'll explain it to you another time. Now I don't have time! Bye! Take care of the children," and he hung up the phone.

Crina, along with her two children, lived close to us and came from time to time to see my wife. Sometimes I helped her with the shopping because she couldn't drive. My wife and Crina got along like two sisters, and as far as I was concerned, the atmosphere in the house was brightened by her free, uncomplicated spirit, which added more gaiety despite her burdened soul. She jokingly said that she was neither in the car nor in the street with Gica, who always told her to be patient. As such, time passed.

I'm not superstitious, but when after dinner one night, Crina investigated my coffee cup and studied the lines written in the dregs on the sides of the cup, she predicted that a big upset was coming to me very soon, and that gave me something to think about. At work, I started more jokingly to throw a wittier word or a compliment to an unmarried colleague, and the girl did not object to an outing with me for lunch at a restaurant or a movie. However, the secretary, an old lady who saw me hugging my colleague in a corner, threatened me to tell Luiza, my wife, everything. The following Sunday, we were invited to a colleague's wedding, and I was afraid that the secretary would talk to my wife. Luiza knew about this wedding and she hardly could wait to go, but I didn't want to. I pretended that I was exhausted from so much work and wanted to rest at home. Luiza got angry, and she used her entire arsenal of arguments to get us to go, but I refused. It was the most terrible argument I had with my wife, and as a result, for about ten days, she didn't talk to me. The secretary never said anything, but out of fear, I started looking for a job elsewhere.

In autumn, on Puiu's birthday, Olga invited us to come on Sunday afternoon to celebrate her husband. After the whole group gathered around the table loaded with good food, Puiu's friend, Nicu, who we knew was their tenant, learned that Crina's husband was in America, and he started to give her a whirl. Amused, I watched his glances and the way he tried to mix in her discussion with other people by inserting views that obviously bothered Puiu, interrupting him too often from telling a story from his arsenal.

"You are saying the same thing that you have told us many times," Olga also intervened.

"It's not true! What do you know about what happened to me? And stop interrupting me, for God's sake!"

"Don't you see that you've bored the world with your stories? Let others talk, too!"

"But let them talk, dear, because I don't stop anyone."

Olga's eyes were lit like headlights, watching the corner where Crina was detained midway by Nicu:

"Crina, do you want to help me bring the cookies to the

table?”

"Of course, my dear. Please excuse me," Crina said to the guy and went into the kitchen after Olga.

I also went in that direction for a glass of water.

"I have the impression that the guy is courting you," I said to Crina, passing by her.

"I have the impression that you are jealous," she answered me with dimples on her cheeks.

"If Gică finds out, you won't laugh like that," Olga intervened seriously.

"Who will tell him? And what exactly?"

"My dear, you know what they say: appearances can easily be taken for truth."

"Really, with whom? With this one? He would be a good man, but I don't think his wife left him for what he was." Crina retorted, not knowing that Nicu had heard everything she said behind her.

"No, my wife didn't let me go as I was. I left her because after she became a department director, I couldn't stand it anymore. Pride, conceit, new claims, and malice. Nothing satisfied her like before. She disliked me, the house, and my job. She starts looking for something else, another advancement, a better position."

"Then, if you don't mind, bring these deserts to the table," Olga told him, putting a plate of cookies in his arms. She also gave Crina a plate.

"I didn't know he was behind me," Crina said when they were alone. "I feel stupid that he heard what I said."

"Don't worry. You forget, he forgets too."

At Christmas, it was our turn to invite. Our children were away with their friends, and Luiza prepared the most delicious dishes all week to prolong the mood until late at night. Crina also helped prepare the feast, and I oversaw last-minute shopping. Crina came with me once to choose what we needed from to buy.

"Do you know anything about Gica?" I asked.

"It's messed up. The woman he met at a bar was underage, and he didn't know. Her parents want to sue him."

"And what is he doing?"

"I don't know. They want him to divorce me and take their daughter as his wife. Otherwise, they'll hand him over to the police. Gica knows she wasn't a virgin, but that doesn't matter."

"And what are you doing?"

"I don't know." Crina started to tear up. "I don't know what to do. It's hard for me, very hard."

I pulled the car over to the side of the road. Crina rested her head on my shoulder, and then I put my arm around her shoulders. She continued to cry without saying anything. I wiped her tears with my handkerchief and kissed her forehead. She pulled me towards her and kissed me on the lips. I knew at that moment that I was opening the gates of a blacker sky than the densest imaginable darkness, but that did not stop me from embracing her, clutching her passionately to my chest. Feeling in my palms her warm, soft relief, I extended the embrace as long as I could.

"I don't know how I'm going to see Luiza after this?" Crina said after I started the engine again.

"I don't know either. All I know is that I want you like crazy."

"Me too."

`When I went to bring Crina home that evening after she let the babysitter go, I stayed with her to discuss the situation. Soon, Luiza called to see if I had left there. We were sitting next to each other on the sofa in the living room. I motioned to Crina to tell Luisa that I was gone. As they continued to talk about the preparations for the party, I knelt at Crina's feet and removed her shoes one by one. Then, caressing her leg, I started pulling her stocking down, ignoring that she was trying to push me away while she was talking to Luiza. But it was too late: Her white flesh imitating the finest marble was too strong a magnet for me to be separated from it. Crina then stood up with the phone in her hand, hurriedly saying to Luiza:

"Forgive me, dear. One of the children is whimpering in the bedroom. I must see what's happening!" Closing the phone, she grabbed it from the table and shoved it hard into my nose:

"You bastard! You take advantage of a moment of weakness, and now you want to rape me in my own home, in front of my children? Aren't you ashamed? Go away! Leave immediately! I don't want to see you again! You are worse than an animal! Get out!"

Laying back on the plush rug in front of the couch, I felt my nose dripping with blood. I was stunned by the radical reversal of the situation. I've never seen Crina so angry. It was useless to try to reconcile her or to say anything. I got up from the floor and touched the doorknob when Crina, still standing, dialed a new phone number:

"Come home right away. If you are not here in two days, you have me on your conscience!" she yelled, red as fire, into the receiver. "I'm throwing myself off the balcony, you know! Or in front of a train. I'll find poison or something else. Two days, because you have children on the way. Do you understand?" And hung up the phone.

When I got home, Luiza was waiting for me. I lingered in the garage, lifting the hood of the car to get my hands dirty.

"Why did it take so long?

"I had problems with the engine. Luckily, a driver stopped and helped me. He unscrewed the spark plugs and cleaned them."

"Good. Go to bed now; it's late."

I went to bed, but I don't think I slept that night. Gica came home two days before Christmas. Crina called Luiza to tell her that she couldn't come; one of the children developed a fever. After the New Year, Luiza told me:

"I don't know what's wrong with Crina. I feel like she's avoiding me. Not only me but others, too. Something is wrong."

I found out later that Gica was looking for another job here in the city. Crina, some say, went into a nervous shock that she doesn't want to see anyone anymore. Towards spring, before Easter, news came that on Sabinelor Street, where Olga and Puiu lived, a man was fatally stabbed with a kitchen knife. It is believed that the act was motivated by the jealousy of the husband, who found his wife in bed with the victim. When asked by the investigators why he did this, the criminal calmly answered:

"He was in my bed. What was he doing there?"

From the description in the papers, it emerged that the victim's name was Niculaie Sărățoiu, Olga's tenant.

The Verdict

"Shit! That's enough for you!"

Sandu had come to pick up his children, left here by his wife Dorina before going to work. On the way home, he stopped by to pick up his mail from the mailbox. Claudia, the neighbor from the 12th floor, had children about the same age as his, and because she didn't work, they agreed to leave the children here until Sandu got home. He found the children watching cartoons on TV stretched out on the living room carpet. Waiting for them, he went through the letters. The neighbor lady passed in front of Sandu to arrange the cushions on the sofa where he was leafing through his letters, and making her way back, she tripped over the coffee table leg and fell into his lap. Shocked seeing her leg like a marble sculpture revealed through the opening of the robe, she got up the next moment saying:

"Shit! That's enough for you!"

Her husband, Ionel, worked at a hotel most of the day. Someone had to stay home with the kids. She was faster with English because she worked in the old country as a saleswoman. However, with the help of a friend, he found a job as a caretaker at a second-rate hotel, and she remained tied to the house and children. With what they received weekly from Dorina and Sandu for the care of the children, they managed.

One day, Claudia said to him, showing him an ad from the newspaper:

"Look, this agency hires the public to watch and choose TV commercials. I will get a hundred dollars for it. Can you stay with the children while I'm gone?"

"Sure. When is it?"

"At six tonight. I called this morning, and I'm on the list. But I need you to take me there by car."

"With the children?"

"Yes. I'll leave you in the car with them, and you can take them to McDonald's."

Luckily, near the hotel where the film screening took place, there was a McDonald's where the children, after eating a burger and fries, could play, and Sandu could take a sip of coffee. After about three hours of waiting, Claudia returned. The children were tired, and when they were put in the back seat of the car, they immediately fell asleep. When they got home, she leaned toward him, kissing his cheek before getting out of the car.

One of the following days, when Sandu went to pick up his children, Claudia prepared two cups of coffee and sat next to him on the sofa:

"Ionel found a used car. He tried it and is good."

"Bravo! You need a car. Without a car, it's hard to get by here."

"Yes, but we don't have enough money."

"How much do you need?"

"I think they ask for twenty-five hundred dollars."

"I'm sorry. We don't have that money."

"I know, but maybe you can sign a guarantee for us."

"Let's see. I also need to talk to Dori, my wife, first."

Claudia started to laugh, hitting him lightly with her elbow between the ribs:

"Stop pretending! What kind of man are you? Do you really have to ask your wife for everything?"

She raised a friendly arm over his shoulder, pressing her breast against his arm. Embarrassed, he did not know what to say. That evening, he told Dorina what Claudia asked him. They decided to guarantee them. They, Ionel and Claudia, also provided them with great service. If they don't help them, who will? they thought. So, they signed.

At the end of the week, Ionel invited them to dinner. They chatted over a glass of wine while the children played in their bedroom. But when they were about to drink coffee, Ionel got a call for an emergency at the hotel. After coffee, Dorina said she wanted to go rest a little, and Sandu stayed with the children to play, giving his wife time to rest quietly at home. Claudia got up to tidy the table, and Sandu helped. In the kitchen, she grabbed his hand:

"Look what the animal did to me."

She lifted her skirt above her knees and showed him the few bruises higher on her thigh:

"He comes home late at night, gets drunk in the kitchen, and then comes to bed. I'm tired, and I want to sleep, but he doesn't understand, he insists, he forces me, and if I resist, he beats me... I can't do it anymore! Ouch, I can't...take it anymore! I want to go back home."

She buried her face in Sandu's chest and started to cry. He put his arms around her protectively and told her to be patient and that everything would work out. Ionel is not a bad man, but he is disappointed. He cannot provide as much as he had back home, and now he suffers. Then, how would she leave without the children? Crying, she clung like a vine tighter to his body as a stable support. Looking helplessly around, he pre-emptively pushed back the kitchen door. Claudia lifted her head, her eyes locked onto his wile she pulled him towards her joining her lips to his in a hungry kiss. He answered.

At home after dinner, helping Dori clean the table while she put the children to bed, Sandu was fiddling with a problem. When Dorina returned to put things in their place, Sandu asked her:

"Why can't we also live normally, like all other people?"

"I had the impression that we were living normally. What does not satisfy you?"

"No, this is not normal! We live by mail. With little notes: buy milk, take out the trash, bathe the children tonight... This is not life! Normal people sleep together, go to work every morning together, come home, and spend the rest of their time together, not apart."

"Do you remember that we discussed this problem? We decided it was better this way. The children were too young for school. Puiu was too small for nursery school, and we could not find a spot for Angela anyway. Maybe in the fall, we'll have better luck."

"I know, but it's hard. I don't like this neighborhood either. We'd better move somewhere else. I want a change."

Dorina hugged him understandingly:

"It will be fine. You will see. Be patient."

When he came home the next day, Sandu found his children playing in the little park between the blocks. Claudia was sitting on a bench crocheting something. Next to her in a nylon bag, the wool thread was untangling from the ball of yarn in the bag. When she saw him, she smiled and made room for him to sit next to her:

"Do you know what I was thinking? It's such a beautiful day. Let us let the kids play here, and we will watch them from your room on the third floor. What do you say?"

"If you have work to do, I can stay here with the children to play."

"No! How am I going to leave you alone? You have not even eaten yet. And then," she said, stroking his leg over his pants: "I want to be close to you. I need your support."

Sandu covered her hand with his palm.

"Claudia, it's not good. I can't be there for you the way you want. I have a wife and children. I cannot, I cannot ruin their lives!"

"No, dear. Don't be like that! Do not make me cry here! You don't understand? You are my only friend. Besides you, I have no one. Come on up!"

Sandu pressed her hand to prevent her from getting up from the bench:

"Wait! Do not press me! Give me time to think. I don't want to complicate our situation. If you want to break up with Ionel, that's your problem. But I love Dori, and I love my kids."

Claudia withdrew her hand from his, called her children, and left, hiding her eyes with her palm. From that day on, whenever he came to pick up his children, Claudia brought them to the door of the apartment without saying a word. This arrangement satisfied Sandu in a way, feeling relieved of the burden of the pressure that had dominated him over since the beginning.

"It's better this way," he told himself with the conviction of one who saw himself rewarded for a righteous decision.

After the Civic Holiday in August, Sandu, Dorina, and the children rented a cottage for a week in the Muskoka Lake region. It felt like paradise for them and for the children. When they returned home to Toronto, the 12th-floor apartment was empty. The tenants had left. They scrambled to find another lady to stay with the children, and life took its course. Towards the end of September, they got a bill in the mail for three hundred dollars a month. They had forgotten that they signed a payment plan for Ionel's car, and no one knew where they went. Even the building manager had no idea where they went because they had debt and damages to pay there, too. Sandu felt guilty because he let himself be deceived by Claudia, who made him pay dearly for his refusal. However, his conscience told him that he did the right thing.

Many years have passed since then. The children were in school now and learning well, and Dorina and Sandu moved to a new house in a residential area. They were satisfied, no longer worked different shifts, and were invited by friends and co-workers to their homes for family events. One Saturday evening, Dorina and Sandu went to the wedding of a friend's daughter. The snow outside made the road almost impassable, and Dorina brought her dancing shoes in a canvas bag to change into at the hall. Hearing them speak Romanian, the wardrobe lady smiled, saying that she was also Romanian, and added:

"You should know that only Romanians, I have observed, come prepared with two pairs of shoes to a party like this."

Sandu put a five-dollar bill in the gratuity cup. In the hall, among the guests gathered to dance in the middle ring, Sandu thought he saw a familiar face:

"Is it possible? Claudia?"

He watched her without saying a word to Dorina, and when he saw Claudia sitting down at a table, he went over. Ionel spots him from a distance, waves to his wife, and then gets up and disappears into the crowd. Claudia got up to meet Sandu, took his arm, smiled, and said:

"Come out to the hall because there is too much noise here. How do you do? Dori and the kids are okay?"

Sandu didn't answer. Claudia brought him to the most secluded corner of the room, next to the wardrobe window that was covered with a plush curtain:

"I know you have reason to be angry. I'm not saying this as an excuse, but I had no choice. We had to do it this way because otherwise, there was no way to finish it. Ionel came first in a violin competition for the Calgary Symphony Orchestra here in Toronto. To get there, we needed money or a car. We had neither and..."

"And then you tried to seduce me."

"No! I loved you. But I had no one to turn to."

"You knew you were going to let me pay your debt, and then you wanted to give yourself to me as a whore. So that you wouldn't owe me anything. Exchange for exchange! No? I wonder if this was also with Ionel's consent?"

An ironic smile bloomed on Claudia's face. She turned her back and walked away towards the hall door but stopped in her tracks and came back to face Sandu, this time ready to attack:

"Are you making me a whore? Come on? Let me show you a whore…"

Her voice rose to a crescendo as she continued:

"You wanted to rape me in my own house! I kept quiet until now so as not to shame you. I didn't even tell my husband, but that's enough! You scoundrel, vicious pervert, if I didn't have a kitchen knife to defend myself, you would have raped me in the kitchen with the kids in the next room, knowing my husband wasn't home.

People, friends, anyone! Look here! This lowest of the low being! I was new to Canada, and this man attacked me in my own home. This pervert assaulted me, knowing that my husband was at work. Look at him and be aware he is shameless. And here, now, he assaulted me again!"

Full of emotion, Claudia finished her monologue crying. The world gathered around, and several came from the reception hall, curious to know what was going on. Ionel appeared from the back of the room, and passing through the crowd, he arrived in front of Sandu. Without a word, he knocked him down with a punch to the face. While Sandu was getting up, someone called the police. Dorina, hearing the commotion in the corridor, also came from the hall and wordlessly tried to get Sandu out of the center of the crowd surrounded by Claudia's cries. Sandu tried to tell the crowd that everything Claudia was saying was pure lies, but no one was willing to listen to him. Arriving at the scene, the police took witness statements, handcuffed Sandu, and dragged him out to the entrance of the hall. At that moment, the wardrobe curtain parted, and the woman attending the coats began shouting in English:

"I heard the whole discussion! This woman is lying! The man spoke the truth; I heard everything said."

The two officers brought Sandu back:

"What did you hear?"

"Everything, from the beginning to the end. She asked him for money and offered him sexual favors in return. He gave her the money but refused her favors. Now she wants revenge!"

"How did you hear? Do you always listen to what people are saying?"

"No. I usually read but they were speaking Romanian, my mother tongue. That caught my attention."

"You must come with us to the police to make a statement."

"I can't now. I must stay here. But tomorrow morning, I can come."

The next day, comments about Sandu's accusation as a sexual predator appeared in newspapers and local television, and as a result, the company he worked for fired him immediately. The judge set a bond for his release from prison at ten thousand dollars, for which Dorina had to take urgent steps to refinance the house. At school, their children were bullied by others for accusations they did not understand. And with the general paranoia fueled by "The Me-Too Movement" in vogue, it was hard to find a defense attorney to support his innocence, especially in the circumstances where there was no witness to the alleged incident in the kitchen long ago. In this situation, will judges give justice to the one who supports his cause more loudly with well-conceived lies, or will it filter the truth through the labyrinth of the judgement of facts, intentions of participating parts, and past behavior?

Until then, however, the inferno of public opprobrium will not be delayed in condemning an innocent family man to the most horrible scrutiny before the verdict.

Crăişor

"I am not your mother; I am your mother's midwife. She gave birth to you; I brought you into the world. It was a big secret because your mother was just a baby when she had you, and then she left you to me, and she went off into her own world. She and her mother sent the carriage for me from a house on the outskirts of the town, and the day after I had you, they left with the Lord. Here is what I have left after they gone."

The old woman took a chain from her neck with a locket hanging from it and passed it over the head of the boy who was sitting on the edge of her bed. She was gasping for breath and struggling to say what she had to say because of the pain that kept her in bed. The boy looked at her with teary eyes, unprepared to learn such strange things about his good mother, who was who knows where, after believing the old woman to be his mother. If this woman who raised and cared for him goes, then to whom does he remain? Who will take care of him?

"I raised you as if you were mine", continued the old woman. "My man - may God forgive him - he didn't really like you at first, but when you grew up a bit, he was proud of you. He called you Crăişor (The Little Prince), and that's how your name remained...: Crăişorul lui Birău. Then the Lord took him from us, and it was just the two of us. I think it is my turn to walk beside him, and I leave you in the care of the Lord, our Christ."

The boy began to cry; the old woman caressed his head and then died, taking with her the last grimace of pain from the old woman's face. She now seemed calm, at peace, as if she was in a beautiful dream.

After she was taken by the people to the pit, everyone went to their homes, and Crăişor was left alone in the empty house. The first few days, he ate everything that could be eaten in the house; he worked with the objects there or outside in the paddock where two goats, a goat, and a heifer, had been in the pen for a few days. When hunger and boredom took him to the village street, he stopped at the fence of Aunt Ileana, who had two children his age in the yard:

"What about you, Crăişor?" asked the aunt.

"I'm hungry!"

"Come to my house, and I'll give you something to eat", said the aunt, opening the gate for him.

She returned after a few minutes with a cube of polenta with plum marmalade on top and a cup of milk. Her children stopped their play and came to watch Crăişor in silence. Their mother looked at them fondly and said:

"Do you see how bad it is not to have a mother?"

After he finished eating, Crăişor thanked the aunty.

"Did you give water to the goats, Crăișor?"

"Oh, no! Mother didn't tell me to," The child confessed.

"Bring them here to me; I will take care of them."

"I'll bring them aunty. But I keep the little goat because he is my friend."

Crăișor took the goats out of the pen and herded them to Aunt Ileana with a stick. On the way back, he had to carry the baby goat in his arms because it didn't want to be separated from its mother. Aunt Ileana's children looked with inquisitive eyes at everything Crăișor did without saying a word. The eyes of those children made him feel awkward, a stranger among them. Loneliness oppressed him as hard as the alienation of those who showed silent pity for him, devoid of warmth. With the goat in his arms, he fell on the bed and covered himself with a blanket. In the middle of the night, he woke up and in the dark. He decided to go somewhere where no one knew him, and he didn't have to know that everyone was watching him.

When it was daybreak, Crăișor put a few things from the house in his bag, made a knot at the end of a rope which he tied around the frail neck of the imp, pulled the door behind him, and went on his way down the village street. After some distance, he was overtaken by a horse-drawn car.

"Mister, will you take me too?"

"Where do you want to go, dude?" the man asked.

"Well, where are you going. To the city."

"I don't go to the town; I stop in the market."

"I'll go to the fair, too, if you take me."

"I'll take you, but what do you want to do with the goat?"

"He's coming with me because he's my friend."

"Well, I can't put him in the car because I have my things there... just hold him in your arms without letting it go."

"I'm holding it, mister. I'm holding it well", said Crăişor, getting in and sitting on the front bench next to the man.

After a short distance, the man stopped the car on the side of the road near a fountain filled with water. He drew water from the well which he overturned in the wooden cart beside the well. Unsaddled the horse, led it to the water, and removed a handful of hay from the car which he placed in front of the horse. Then he sat down in the shade, taking out a loaf of bread and a piece of bacon from the bag, which he cut into small slices with his knife. Seeing Crăişor, who was looking at him while stroking the rump of his little goat, the man shared some of his food. Shortly after, they continued down the road.

In the crowded fair, the peasants' carts lined up along a vacant lot at the side of the road. Rows of stalls formed passageways for shoppers hurrying to find needed merchandise. The noise amazed Crăișor, who was not used to scenes of this kind. The man also took his car to the roadside and brought it out to display his goods kept cool under the straw in the car. He had butter wrapped in vine leaves, cheese, a dollop of cream, and another with milk for sale.

"You don't want to sell me your goat?" the man asked.

"I can't because he's my friend," answered Crăișor.

"And now, what are you doing here?"

"I'm going to the road. Maybe someone will take me to town."

"Okay, that's it. In the evening, I go home if you want to go with me."

"I don't know. Let me see, mister. Thanks for the ride!"

Crăișor left the fare and went to the main road, on which chariots, carts, carriages, and cars travelled in the rush from all directions. As he was walking along the road with his goat pulled by the rope behind him, a truck, attracting the attention of an incoming driver, honked his horn loudly, and the frightened goat freed itself from the child's hand and ran into the middle of the road. Crăișor went after him to catch him, but a car coming from behind hit him, knocking him a good distance onto the cobblestone pavement of the road. The child was rushed to the nearest hospital in the city, where it was found that despite the terrible blow, only a few bones were broken, with a chance of full recovery. On the operating table, a doctor found the medallion around Crăişor's neck. Inlaid on it was the princely engraving of the noble Calimachi family, and immediately after leaving the hall, he telephoned the family about the condition of the injured child. A short time after, Princess Calimachi, accompanied by her husband, came to the hospital, saw Crăişor still sleeping in his bed, and fainted.

Mr. Bratu

Mr. Bratu did not tie his cravat around his neck today. He didn't even put on his shoes, usually mirror-polished. He remained in his slippers and shirt's collar, left unbuttoned. For thirty years or more, day after day, he wore his cravat around his neck and his coat on his shoulders, whether it was hot or cold, winter or summer, whether he was at home or at work.

Today, however, something was different. It's hard to explain but today is not like other days. Usually, at fifteen minutes past six, he would automatically jump out of bed, do his toiletries, making sure his face was perfectly shaved, his hair combed with a parting in the middle, and his nails neatly trimmed. Then he would go down to the kitchen where he would prepare his breakfast, which consisted of two eggs boiled for two minutes and thirty seconds, with two slices of bread passed through the electric toaster to a tawny color, on which he would spread as much butter as could fit on the tip of a knife. A cup of filtered coffee with a splash of milk in it completed the menu. He would scan over the headlines of the morning paper which he subscribed to, while he ate. Then, at exactly fifteen minutes past seven, he would leave his house, taking his Borsalino hat and umbrella from the hanger by the door. From the corner of the street, he would take the bus that crossed the city to the center. For thirty years or more, things repeated themselves exactly like clockwork, day in and day out, without deviation from the established pattern that, for him, meant the letter of the law, pride, and comfort.

Except today. At the shrill sound of the clock indicating fifteen minutes past six, Mr. Bratu did not jump out of bed, even though he was not sick, he had no pain or even a bad dream to disturb his sleep. He simply stared at the ceiling for another half hour. In the toilet, after he had lathered his face well with shaving cream when he picked up the razor, he looked at its gleaming blade ready for action, then he toweled off his face and put it back the razor. He dressed leisurely and took the tie out of its usual holder to put it around his neck but changed his mind and hung it back. In the kitchen, he absentmindedly took out the pot in which he boiled his eggs in the morning, but instead of putting water in it, he poured milk. Instead of toast and coffee, he took a box of oatmeal, his late mother's favorite, and a jar of honey from the cupboard. The newspaper today has been left on the doorstep, and it sat there all day. He ate absentmindedly, chewing the porridge from his plate for a long time, then got up to go back to his bedroom. To begin with, he sat down in the plush armchair the color of ripe plums that matched the curtains of the window where he could look out at the leafless trees on which traces of snow from the previous days' snowfall were still visible. He then noticed that on one of the bedside tables, his father's framed photograph was dangerously close to the edge, and he went to secure it in the center next to the silk-shaded lamp. In the photograph, a wiry man dressed in a black suit with a waistcoat stood majestically in a statuesque position, exuding plenty of energy and dignity. His father's gaze fixed on the magical eye of the camera was poignant, as was his arched black mustache over his lips. Mr. Bratu admired his father's photo for a long time with regret that the man in it was no longer there today when a piece of his advice could open new perspectives, easing the confusion about the problem that arose unexpectedly on this day. Mr. Bratu's whole life followed the principles of his father who served as his model in every action he undertook down to the smallest details.

Spartan-like discipline, the rigor of fulfilling daily duties, punctuality, and honoring the truth were the cardinal principles by which he led himself in life. He was taught by his father that in the complex gears of life, he was but a mere cog, like those in a clock, having a precise role in that mechanism. To make it more convincing, his father would take out his pocket watch in his palm with the back cover open, showing his son the wheels inside, engaged in rhythmic movement coordinated by an oscillator.

"Without these cogs, one of which is you, the mechanism cannot function, with all the force stored in the coil of the spring inside. Just as that little wheel in the clock is indispensable to its proper functioning, so are you in society," said his father.

With a sigh, he got up from the armchair and went to the room where his father would do his calculations at the polished walnut desk in front of the window facing the street. He pulled open one of the drawers and took out the gilt-capped watch. On the front cover, engraved in cursive letters, was the dedication from the company where his father had worked for four decades. Mr. Bratu opened the back cover of the watch. None of the gears were turning. He wound the knob a few times to engage the spring but to no avail. He shook it nervously and tapped it lightly against the edge of the desk, with no result. He tossed it back into the drawer and muttered to himself:

"Who needs it anymore when there are electronic watches everywhere? Electronic watches don't have gears and complicated mechanisms."

Outside the window, he saw children absorbed in play on their mobile phones and thought:

"Cogs and gears are no longer necessary. I was let go because, in today's virtual - electronic world, I'm no longer useful. These kids on the street were born in this world. The gear-driven world is no longer in fashion. The virtual - electronic world has taken its place.

Nela

"Where are you going now?"

"I have to go to the bank to withdraw some money, and then I want to go home and take a bath because I've been wearing the same shirt for three days, and I can't take it anymore."

"It will take too long, and I don't know why today I have a bad feeling; I am afraid of something. I think I had a bad dream last night, but I don't remember what."

"What can happen? I see you're looking better now after the operation. And the pain seems to show less."

"Yes, but it is from morphine."

I sat in the balance: to leave or not? Poor woman. Nela, my wife of over 40 years, has cancer and was operated on a week ago. I stayed with her here in this hospital room day and night. I felt sorry for her, and I hoped for a miracle, even though the doctor told me yesterday that she wouldn't get better. Her cancer progressed too far; it metastasized throughout her body, and there was nothing they could do for her. With the current pandemic problems that made everyone crazy, the hospital doesn't have enough beds for Covid patients who crowed the emergency rooms. He said I must take her home.

"Yes, but what can I do with her when she is in pain? Do you know how awful it is to see her crying next to me, asking to do something for her, and I can't do anything? Doc, please, don't send her home yet; let her stay here in the hospital where she feels safe under your care."

"I don't know, it doesn't depend on me. Hospital policy is to send the terminally ill home. Your wife is not getting better."

"Please, I beg you, not yet."

"I don't know. Let's see."

Three days had passed since then. Nela, from the bed, looked at the beautiful sunny day at the end of winter and calmly caressed my hand held in hers. Weak beyond recognition in recent weeks since the cancer was discovered, there were times when she thought there may be a chance for recovery because I had not yet told her what the doctors said to me. What was the point of telling her? While she was here in the hospital, her life could be extended a few weeks, even months. All I had to do was to inspire her confidence that everything would end well, and for that, it was necessary to play the part of one who does not care about anything bad. Withdrawing my hand from hers, I stood up:

"I must go now, Nela. I have no money left; last night, I spent the last penny on that donation box after I got cookies for the night shift staff here."

When I was about to take my coat off the back of the chair, Nela looked me in the eyes as if she wanted to make sure I wasn't lying to her and asked:

"But are you coming back soon?"

"Of course, dear. As fast as I can."

As I passed by the nursing station, the nurse who took care of Nela came to inform me that she had received instructions today that Nela would be discharged.

"But that's not possible. When I talked to the doctor, he promised me that he would try to keep her. Where is he now?"

"I don't know," the nurse told me. "I have to draw up the respective forms."

Instead of going to the bank, I started looking for the doctor through all the hospital rooms on the floor. It was hard to search for him. In the rooms where patients lay behind long blue plastic curtains that surrounded the beds, I stood to listen for the voices of those who were talking behind them. From a room I finally heard the doctor's voice and waited until he finished his patient visit.

"Doctor, the nurse told me that today you want to discharge my wife home."

"Yes, we can't keep her in the hospital anymore."

"Doctor, please, I'm not ready today. I stayed with her the

whole time here in the hospital. Taking her home, I need a day or two to clean up. I can't bring her in there like this; I will throw her into depression if she sees what's there. Please, doctor, I beg you."

"I don't know. Let me see what I can do. But only until tomorrow!"

"Until tomorrow. God bless you! Thank you, doc!"

I went back to Nela, who looked at me in amazement:

"Did you finish so quickly?"

"No, I didn't even leave. Today, they wanted to send you home. I talked to the doctor to keep you here at least until tomorrow. I am now going to prepare everything necessary. I have to do some shopping because we have no food in the fridge. I'll see you when I'm done."

"Okay, but don't do anything more than what's necessary. You must take care of yourself, too."

"I will. Don't be afraid. I want to talk to one of the nurses to come to you once a day."

"Why?"

"Well, to let her see you, give you your injections and everything you need."

"Yes, but that costs a lot."

"It's okay, don't be afraid... It's going to be fine!"

I left. Nela watched me until I walked out the door. Dear Nela, she is so warm and sincere; I always had a guiding angel by my side with her, ready to sacrifice herself for my well-being. Lately, the thought that I would soon lose her and be alone was weighing heavily on my shoulders, and I could not perceive the situation as a possibility. What would I do when I'll be without her? How would I be able to spend the rest of my days alone without feeling Nela next to me? Without listening to her voice? And without her caresses that have warmed our hearts for more than forty years of marriage? No, it was not an easy thing to conceive. Thinking all this while I drive, my eyes filled with tears. A lump in my throat prevented me from breathing, and I stopped at the edge of the curb. Here I was alone; I didn't have to hide my pain, and I didn't have to play the hero's confidence in a happy conclusion. Now I could cry release my pain and all the hopeless thoughts of the impending loss. At least these last precious moments that we could spend together must be joyful. I could make her happy and brighten her soul to reduce her suffering.

I turned on the engine and entered the bank. From there I went to a supermarket and bought food I knew she liked. Then I went home. I tidied, vacuumed, and arranged everything the way I knew Nela liked. In the end, I realized I forgot to buy flowers. Flowers were always one of her favorite things. If she didn't have at least one vase of fresh flowers in the house, to her, it seemed that everything in her house was crying. I moved my wedding ring to my right hand so I wouldn't forget to go buy flowers too.

In the evening, after cooling off with a shower at home, I went to the hospital again. I arrived in Nela's room. Her bed was empty, and the sheets changed. None of Nela's belongings were left in her room, no medicine, no cell phone with a red cover, and no clothes worn the day she came to the hospital. I went to find one of the nurses:

"Where did you move my wife?

"Just a moment, please. What's her name?

"Ionela Marinescu."

"Ionela? I'm sorry, she passed away today. She's down at the morgue."

"How is it possible? She was okay today when I left?"

"As I said, I'm sorry, she died."

"You cannot! You killed her. She couldn't die suddenly like that."

"Don't talk to me like that! Her cancer could no longer be treated. There was no hope for her."

"But this is no reason for her to be killed by the hospital."

"Who says we killed her?"

"I say! I want to talk to the doctor!"

"He's not here. He went home!"

"Then someone else. The Director."

"At this time, there is no one. Listen to me: go home. Tomorrow, you will receive a legal report with the cause of death. You can chat with whoever you want tomorrow. Now it's too late, and nothing can change anyway. Your wife is no more."

I was leaning over the nursing desk counter and felt like I couldn't keep standing on my feet. Everything had become clear to me: the nurse from the evening shift, not knowing what I discussed with the doctor in the morning, to comply with the orders, administered an increased dose of morphine to Nela. That finished her. A lost life for a bed reserved for another condemned to die.

The Glasses

"What are you looking for?"

"I cannot find my glasses..."

"Well, where did you remove them from your eyes?"

"I don't know..."

"Where could they be?... Now, when I want you to see what is written on this medicine label... Step aside so I can see if you didn't leave them in the bathroom or bedroom..."

"Stop. I think I left them in the kitchen...They steamed when I opened the oven door to see if the pie was browned."

"Come on! I've been sitting with these pills in my hand for so long! I need to see what side effects they have. All these directions are written in such small letters that I don't know if anyone can read them..."

"Give them to me, dear, so I can see what it says."

I took the medicine container from my wife's hand and sat under the chandelier in the kitchen so I could better see the writing. I admit, the fine print was hard to decipher, and it didn't say anything about side effects anyway. I took out the sheet of paper from inside the box, and there, in equally small letters in all the languages of the earth, I found a paragraph that frightened me with several contraindications to be avoided.

"Why do they put it out on the market if the medicine can kill you in all these cases?" I thought.

My wife gloomily listened to the litany of contraindications, trying to weigh whether it was worth taking the medication or not. For a while, my poor wife began to distrust doctors and medicine, especially after she almost lost her voice due to prolonged use of a drug that permanently damaged her thyroid gland and who knows what else. Any new medicine prescribed by the family doctor was passed through a vigorous re-evaluation process, which in the end regarded me in the position of a supreme judge to decide if is better to use it, or not:

"Well, dear, what can I say? If your doctor prescribed it and considering the tiny amount of this harmful ingredient, I'd say...you know...it may be fine to take it, but..."

"Blah, blah, blah... that is how you are. By the time you decide to answer a simple question, the summer is over. Better I'll wait for Lili. She will come to us today, and she knows because she's a nurse."

"Lily? The one who buried two men and is now working on the third? Do you put her in front of the doctor who prescribed your medicine?"

"Yes! Because she has experience. She has worked in the hospital all her life and knows..."

"It's your business, but I wouldn't trust her..."

"Then who should I ask?"

"I think Sofi. She is more calculated; she judges before she speaks, and she doesn't tell you to do what she says."

"Ah, Sofi, always your Sofi...I don't know what you found in her. I don't like her at all. When you look at her, she doesn't even look like a woman; dry as she is she looks more like a mummy. What is your attraction to this woman?"

"Not one."

"You lie to me! I know you..."

"Are you crazy? After all these years?"

"No! Don't tell me I don't know you...I always knew..." and suddenly she started to cry.

I stared at her dumbfounded, not understanding anything. Then, the doorbell rang, and I rushed to open the door. It was Lily. Sensing from afar that she had struck at the wrong moment, she broke the silence like a trumpet in the stillness of the night.

"What's with you? Did you fight again?"

"No, dear. My husband started to glorify Sofi..."

"And what's wrong about that?"

"She thinks I have nothing better to do than go after her..." I answered her.

"And isn't it true?"

"No! Where did you get this idea? You know how she is, depress and with low esteem. I may have paid her a compliment once, but that doesn't mean that..."

"Well, you gave me a compliment, too! Do you remember? While you were holding my shoulders in the car with one hand, you were pecking me like a chicken with the other hand..."

"I? Did I do this? You are confusing me with someone else..."

"It doesn't matter now! Thirty years have passed since then. But I'm not in the habit of confusing anyone."

"I knew! I knew! That's how it's been with me all my life... I'm curious to know if he is the same now, in old age..."

"Now? Who will look at him now? Forgive him, and that's it..."

After pie and coffee, Lili said her goodbyes and went home. It was her birthday; her seventies, and who knows how many more years over. Left alone, my wife followed me, spinning around the house:

"What are you looking for?"

"The glasses. I don't know where I left them..."

"Well, where did you take them off your eyes?"

"That's it! I don't know..."

The Visit

No, today's visit from his sister-in-law Carmen, was not what he supposed it would be, a pleasant visit. On the contrary, Carmen came determined to show the cards face up, and she did it.!

"Don't you see, sister, that he is lying to you? Are you stupid, or what is wrong with you? Your daughter has been dead for seven years, and he tells you that she is somewhere in a sanatorium in America. Do you believe him? It has been seven years since you last saw her! Do you still believe his lies?"

"No! Don't say that! Tony is not lying! He never lied to me! Why would he do it now?" asked Daniela.

"To protect you! Why do you believe Dinu came here from Canada seven years ago? Why do you think he came? Because Sandra went into a coma after heart surgery. Yes, that is what happened: after being in a coma for a week, she died. She was buried before Good Friday."

Daniela could no longer hold back her tears. Standing frozen in the middle of the living room of her apartment, caught off guard by the gravity of what Carmen said, she felt the need to lean on something and approached the couch against the wall. Carmen was still standing watching her older sister. Without saying a word, Tony sat down on the chair by the door, looking down at the floor.

"To protect me? How can you protect someone in the face of death?" she asked. "Is it true what Carmen says?" she asked Tony.

The man put his head in his hands and did not answer his wife. What could he say to her? With her heart weakened after going through so much after a life full of bitterness, poverty, and war, when he saw that the doctors no longer gave him any hope that Sandra would come out of the coma, he decided that it was better to keep the secret of the child's death. Daniela already had complications with her fragile heart and was afraid that she would not be able to endure such terrible news. Dinu, their eldest son, who came from Canada upon receiving the news that his sister was in a coma at the hospital, together with Bogdan, Sandra's husband, and their daughter Alina, decided not to say anything to the mother. The funeral took place quietly at the cemetery with the participation of family members, work colleagues, and acquaintances. Everyone understood why Daniela was not supposed to know the truth and the secret was kept until now.

At first, Daniela felt her knees bending on their own and let herself fall, guided by the edge of the sofa, onto the cushion. She cried silently, with her nose buried in a handkerchief held in the palm of her hand. She had a hunch that something was wrong with her dear girl, Sandra, but the cheerfulness with which Tony told her how lucky they were as Dinu had a doctor friend at Loma Linda Sanatorium in California and managed to get Sandra a place there.

That worked like a miracle, and in the rush to leave, there wasn't even time to say goodbye to everyone. Dinu stayed connected with Sandra by phone, and she told him that she received excellent care. Of course, Daniela missed Sandra immensely and it was hard for her without her by her side. If she could, she would have gone there to see her, but the distance was too great, and she could no longer endure a long journey. At least it was good that she had Alina here, Sandra's little girl, who had just finished high school and was about to enter university. God, when did all these years go by, and how did she allow herself to delusion to think that Sandra was somewhere so far away without receiving a letter, a phone call, or a sign that she was alive? Was that stupidity a sign of dementia or senility? It was the desire to push the pain away, to keep it at bay, knowing that one day it would get to her, but not yet. She knew all along, but she didn't have the courage to tell herself...

Carmen sat next to her sister, trying to ease her pain by brushing her bleached hair that covered her shoulders. In the small living room of the apartment, where the daylight had begun to gradually decrease as evening fell, the distance between the souls of the three of them seemed to have grown as if each of them had moved to other realms. The passion of each of them was different; their regrets were not the same and inexplicable; there were no words to motivate their actions, which further distanced them in these moments when a hug would have been the closest cure. Faced with this sight, Carmen felt guilty, outraged at herself for what she had done, and seeing that her intervention did not help anyone in any way, she began to cry as well.

After a while, Daniela put her arm around her shoulders, holding her lightly to her chest, and kissed her on the face without saying a word. She got up from the couch and headed to the kitchen. A square of sharp-angled light spread across the living room carpet as she turned the knob on the electrical switch. As if awakened from a trance, Tony got up from his chair and followed her, stopping at the kitchen door:

"Would you like to go tomorrow morning to Sandra with a flower?" he asked.

"I don't think so. Tomorrow, I want to buy wheat for coliva (the Romanian funeral wheat porridge). We will bring it to the church on Sunday to be sanctified by the priest; then we will go to see Sandra.

Carmen also came into the kitchen, approaching her sister:

"Do you forgive me for telling you?"

Daniela lingered for a moment in front of Carmen. The beads of tears glistened in her eyes. She hugged her once more. Suddenly, her eyes widened as if a vision appeared before her:

"I have to wear mourning clothes, and I don't have a

dress...Sandra - God, forgive me! – my little girl was not treated properly by her mother."

Carmen supported Daniela by the shoulders, trying to calm her sister:

"No, it's not your fault. If you want, I'll give you my mourning dress. But I don't think you should wear it now."

"No! The tradition must be preserved! I will keep mourning all year! Sandra has already suffered enough from the neglect."

Daniela broke away from Carmen and approached the stove where the kettle had started to boil. On the table in the center of the room, she arranged cups, saucers, the sugar box, and a plate with butter and cheese sandwiches. Tony pulled out a chair and motioned for Carmen to sit down. Then he took Daniela's hand, and together, they crossed the threshold of the balcony door where the evening was cool under the dome of twinkling stars. The moon glided smoothly over the luminescent ice of the clouds like a silent swan. Tinted silvery reflections covering everything from trees, walls, the ground and the people, the night breathes peace and harmony.

Sweetheart

These days, when she sees me settle in with the laptop on my lap, she knows I need quiet and retreats to her room. Our shared space—the living room—has become uncomfortable for both of us. I'm not naturally grumpy, but I'm not one for long phone conversations, asking friends what they're up to, what news they've heard from others, or any of that chit-chat. Sweetheart—that is, my lifelong wife—on the other hand, has found her true mission in such things. In fact, when the phone rings, I don't even bother picking it up anymore; I let her answer. No one ever calls me anyway. But Sweetheart—she's always on the line, no matter the hour, the day, or even the holiday. That's why, for some peace and quiet, I turn to my laptop.

But I shouldn't be unfair. At our age, holed up in a small apartment with nothing much to do beyond our daily routine, what else is there? When the weather's nice, we sit on the balcony and watch the street life below: cars buzzing by, people scurrying about like ants, the sunset slipping behind the rooftops in the distance. It's not much different from the way our elders used to do it, gazing from a bench beside the old village fence, watching the young folk bustle or the children play. After dinner, once it's dark, I turn on the TV to see what's going on in the world. If Sweetheart notices I'm more interested in the newscasters than in what she wants to talk about, she gets upset and withdraws to her room again. From there, I hear her calling her friends and chatting away until sleep finally comes.

Lately, Sweetheart and I have pretty much run out of things to talk about. Even our memories have turned into points of contention:

"Do you remember what my uncle gave us as a wedding present?"

"Uncle Costică from Caracal? Advice."

"What do you mean, advice? Are you saying my uncle didn't give us anything?"

"He did—advice! Told us to buy a Fram fridge, said he'd just got one and it was solid."

"No. I clearly remember he gave us a thousand lei."

"Nonsense! That wasn't him. That was your father who gave us the money. Your uncle showed up empty-handed, just full of hot air. No one could get a word in with him around. A fridge, really? When didn't we even have a place to live? If it hadn't been for my folks giving up their bedroom for us, you'd still be living at your mother's."

"That's just like you—always ungrateful. You only ever praise your side of the family…"

"Well, isn't it true?"

"There you go again, always trying to put me down with remarks like that, as if you're the only one who remembers anything. You know what? It's better if people don't talk to you at all!" said Sweetheart, storming off to her room.

Left alone and full of regret for upsetting her once again, I opened the laptop, which lit up, delighted to have my attention. Sometimes I'm stirred by the urge to shape thoughts into words, into verse, once appreciated by a few friends and acquaintances. But not always. Sometimes I sit there, face-to-face with the screen, tired of waiting, and when it dims, as if it too might abandon me, I stroke its sensitive little spot with my middle finger, and it lights up again, pleased.

Still, when no idea comes to mind, as though the emptiness inside me lets no echo escape—I feel like a vacant nest under the eaves after the birds have flown. Worried that yet another window is closing to me, like so many others since crossing the threshold into retirement, I can find no comforting explanation to chase the fear away. I tell myself this isn't a sign of senility, just loneliness— a lack of activity and connection with people still engaged in life's machinery. That's where the remedy lies! If water at the bottom of a well isn't drawn, it stagnates and dries up. I have to get out more! I tell myself. I need to go to the mall, the park, to strike up conversations, exchange ideas. But where would I do that? With whom? Who has time to chat with me? Even my own kids don't have time, and when they do, I know they're keeping their troubles from me, so I won't worry.

"Hey, buddy," I tell myself, "Can't you see you missed the train? Go back to your quiet little corner and enjoy the sunset view."

Disheartened, I leave the laptop and head toward Sweetheart's room. Suspicious, she tells the person on the phone she'll call them back and looks at me, concerned.

"What's wrong? Are you feeling okay?"

"No… I'm bored. I've got no one to talk to…"

"But you don't like talking."

"Me? Come on, when we have company or go to a party, am I not the one who livens up every conversation?"

"Sure, but you don't talk—you preach. What do you actually know about the people you talk to? Who comes to you and says they've got a problem? Who do you try to help with what you can, or with a kind word?"

"No, my dear. You're wrong there! I've never turned down anyone who's come to me for help… You know I've helped so many people."

"That's true, but they didn't come to you. They came to me. They opened up to me, and when they needed help, we did what we could—together. You're not unkind… just distant. Cold."

That was more than enough of a conversation with Sweetheart. I went back and gently touched the laptop's glowing face, happy to breathe life into strings of letters lined up like soldiers on parade. And at the head of them all, in proud, elegant capitals, I wrote the title that let the world read the word SWEETHEART.

The Choosing

One midday, as the sun sat high and hot above the world, three men appeared at the entrance of my tent—bearded, robed in garments the colour of snow. I stepped out and bowed deeply to welcome them and implored them to honour my humble shelter with their presence. A maidservant brought forth a basin of water, and kneeling before them, I washed and dried their feet. Then, laying before them my finest fare, I invited them to eat, to rest, to recover from the long road they had travelled.

"How fares the good man of this tent?" asked the one in the centre, who seemed to be the elder among them.

"Well, what can I say?" I replied. "So long as the pasture is green and my sheep are well, praise be to the Lord for His mercy!"

"Indeed," he said. "But you must know these things do not last."

"You speak the truth, my Lord. I see the black clouds gathering above and, in my heart, I fear the storm that will surely descend upon us. Messengers have brought news from afar—of a world fallen into wickedness, of a Law forgotten, and of Lies held in higher regard than Truth. I fear, my Lord, the wrath that comes, and I pray for forgiveness—ours and that of our children."

The three strangers listened in solemn silence. Then the one seated to the right spoke:

"How do you know what is true? When one accuses another of wrongdoing, and the accused points right back to his accuser—how can one judge rightly between them?"

"I cannot say," I answered. "If I do not know the root of their quarrel, I do not know to whom justice belongs."

"Let us imagine," the man continued, "that the accuser had given the accused a gold coin to settle a debt at the marketplace the following day. On the road, the accused is robbed by bandits. Upon his return, he claims he could not pay the debt, for he was waylaid. There are no witnesses. What then? Who is right?"

"The accused," I replied. "He faced the danger. The same fate might have befallen the accuser had he walked that road instead."

"But now suppose," the man said slowly, "that someone saw the accused feasting and drinking with a friend at the market, showing not a trace of distress over any supposed robbery…"

"Ah!" I exclaimed. "Then the matter changes! Surely the accuser is in the right—he has suffered twice: first the loss of his gold, and still remains in debt to the merchant. The accused is a base and wretched thief."

"But" added the man, "the witness who claimed to have seen

him reveling in the market is known to all as a liar and a scoundrel, a man who would sell even his own mother for gain. When pressed by the elders of the city, he confessed to having lied."

"Lord in Heaven," I breathed, shaken by the image of such depravity. The three strangers watched me in quiet expectation, waiting for my judgment.

"Noble guests," I said at last, "this is a heavy burden to weigh. But I believe the accused should return the gold coin to the accuser, for the loss was not of the latter's doing. Beyond that, I do not know what to say."

The old man on the far left spoke at last:

"You have judged wisely, good man. In His great wisdom, the Lord has brought us to your tent. These days, few remain among the Chosen, for lies, lawlessness, and sin have stretched across the earth. The sheep of the Lord are abandoned; the shepherds, drawn into temptation, have forsaken their calling. The Lord is grieved by what has come to pass, and the signs of His wrath, which should strike fear into every heart, are ignored by men. Evil must be uprooted, and many will pay the price."

"Mercy, Lord!" I cried. "Have mercy on the innocent! Do not let Thy sorrow visit ruin upon those who have done no wrong. Forgive, O Lord, those who have kept Thy commandments, those who have hoped in Thee, knowing they could not stop the evil, and forgive the weak, who fell to the seduction of lying tongues! Have mercy, Lord, for they know not what they do…"

"If you believe they are worthy of the Lord's mercy," said the elder, "then gather your children, your grandchildren, your household, your servants, and your flocks. Set your face toward the place where the sun rises—toward the tallest mountain of them all. There, build a temple upon the summit, for that is what the Lord commands. People will ask why you do this. You shall say, 'The Lord has called me to raise His house on high.' Some may follow you. Your kin may call you mad. Many will mock you, and your enemies will curse and hurl stones after you. But all those who do not follow of their own will shall perish when the Lord breaks the dams and the waters rise to flood the world."

"But Lord," I said, "why me? Could you not find another more worthy? I am old and frail. My strength is gone with the passing of my good years. My legs fail me, my voice falters, my eyes dim, and even my thoughts betray me. How shall I fulfill this task?"

"You are the Chosen," he replied. "Your feet will find the path. Your voice will be heard by great and small. Your eyes shall see as the eagle sees from above. And your mind shall be keen, as in the days of your youth."

"Lord, have mercy on your servant! Mercy, O Lord!" I cried,

falling face-first to the ground before the three.

When I lifted my head, the light of morning had filled the room. Through the open window, the chirping of birds poured in along the sun's first rays of the day, after the dream of the night before. How strange was this vision... I shall not listen to the news before bedtime ever again.

About The Author

Born in Bucharest, Romania, in January 1934, David Kimel witnessed the changes and turmoil of his country, dragged by forces beyond its control in the era preceding, during, and after the Second World War. Raised on the periphery of the city, surrounded by poor to middle-class neighbors, he learned at an early age the existence of prejudice, the lessons of survival which kept his Jewish family afloat through tough times, and gave him the strength to grow as a man.

After finishing an industrial school, he was selected by the Romanian Writers Union in 1952 for a scholarship at "Şcoala de Literatură şi Critică Literară Mihail Eminescu," an eminent literary academy for young writers, where he had the opportunity to meet the most prominent writers as teachers and colleagues. But he couldn't satisfy the regime's requirements and found work in industry. He married, had children, and immigrated to Canada in 1975, after a waiting period of eight months for the visa in Greece refugee camp.

In his new country, he finally got a designer job with Magna International, a multinational company for automotive parts, where he held a leading position until retirement. He started to write again when his children became young adults. Among the many publications where he began collaborating, *Observatorul* (The

Observer), a Romanian magazine in Toronto, created a permanent column, "Subjective," where his articles have appeared regularly for almost 20 years.

Many books in English and Romanian featuring his name have been printed since 2008. Among them, *Simple Seeds*, a poetry book printed by Author House, and *A Foggy Sunrise*, published by iUniverse. Two other books, *A Sweetless Love* and *In the Pursuit of Happiness*, are presently published by Paramount Book Publishing. In Romanian, David Kimel brought to light the novels: *Domnița și Tudor Avădanei* and *Capcana*; the short story collections *În Căutarea Fericirii* and *Anișoara*; a book of poems, *Flori de Toamnă*; a memoir, *Zori Încețoșate*; a travelogue, *Din Lumea Largă*; and a collection of published articles, *Disecarea Timpului Prezent*.

David Kimel is a member of the Romanian Writers Association of Canada (ASRC), the Writers and Editors Network, and the recipient of a Second Prize in the International Competition of Saga Printing House for the short story titled *Domnul Bratu*.